LIZ MILLER

Sunrises and Sagebrush

A quirky, spicy retelling of Pride and Prejudice

Copyright © 2025 by Liz Miller

All rights reserved. No part of this publication may be reproduced, stored or transmitted in any form or by any means, electronic, mechanical, photocopying, recording, scanning, or otherwise without written permission from the publisher. It is illegal to copy this book, post it to a website, or distribute it by any other means without permission.

This novel is entirely a work of fiction. The names, characters and incidents portrayed in it are the work of the author's imagination. Any resemblance to actual persons, living or dead, events or localities is entirely coincidental.

Liz Miller asserts the moral right to be identified as the author of this work.

Designations used by companies to distinguish their products are often claimed as trademarks. All brand names and product names used in this book and on its cover are trade names, service marks, trademarks and registered trademarks of their respective owners. The publishers and the book are not associated with any product or vendor mentioned in this book. None of the companies referenced within the book have endorsed the book.

First edition

This book was professionally typeset on Reedsy.
Find out more at reedsy.com

Contents

1	Sunrises	1
2	Sagebrush	5
3	Meet Cute	11
4	Vision	17
5	Grit and Determination	20
6	Offbeat	24
7	Un-Phased	29
8	Catching Crushes	34
9	Just a Fence	37
10	Keep It Cool	42
11	Meet Not-Cute	47
12	Certified? Or Certifiable	50
13	Reinforcements Arrive	54
14	Chop Wood, Carry Water	62
15	Wine Walk	68
16	Barbecued	77
17	Oh, Right…	86
18	The Morning After	91
19	No Big Deal	95
20	Progress	99
21	The Anniversary	103
22	The Girlfriend	106
23	Hello, Butterflies	111
24	Talk About a Dom	117
25	Slow Burn Manipulation	122
26	You Remind Me of the Babe	129

27	Gilded Guilt	132
28	Blue-Eyed Devil	137
29	Homecoming	140
30	Chocolate Lasagna	144
31	It's Not a Date	149
32	Dirty Dancing	154
33	So Done	159
34	Puppy Love	163
35	No More Games	168
36	The Letter	171
37	Broken Fences	174
38	Mending Fences, Building Bridges	179
39	An Actual Date	183
40	Stealth is My Talent	189
41	Stay	193
42	Taboo, or Not Taboo	195
43	A Girl and Her Horse	199
44	This One's Got Heart	203
45	A Moment In the Sun	208
46	Party Planner Extraordinaire	210
47	It's Happening For Real	213
48	Something Real	217
49	Another Sunrise	220
50	Epilogue	223

One

Sunrises

Beth

My hair whips across my face for the third time—wild brown curls catching in my mouth like tumbleweeds. I spit one out and curse under my breath.

"Woa, girl!" I pull up on Gypsy's reins as I fish strands from my mouth. Glasses I should have left at home slide down my nose again, and I push them up with the back of my glove.

Spring in Nevada. I'd forgotten just how windy it gets at the base of the Sierra Nevada mountain range. I do my best to twist my Medusa's mane up into a knot but it's ultimately a futile effort as the wind works relentlessly against me. Gypsy stomps and scoots her butt sideways impatiently.

"Fine, fine, you guys win," I say to both the horse and Mother Nature.

I give up on my hair and guide Gypsy through the sea of sagebrush as it begins to give way to intermittent pine trees. Living in a high desert at the foot of an alpine mountain range is a unique experience. In early spring, there's still snow up on the mountain, but down here, the valley floor is dry and brown, just beginning to wake up.

As we clear a copse of pines, I get a clear view of the rising sun over the foothills on the east end of the Carson Valley. Well, kind of clear, except for the brown curls that whip like Medusa's snakes, nipping at my eyes.

Still, it's a damn beautiful view. Pale yellow beams of light cut through the calm baby blue of the morning sky and illuminate puffy clouds across the horizon. There's a chill in the air but I already feel the warmth of the sun's rays, burning through it. Today will be a warm day.

It feels nice to get out for an extended ride, and Gypsy seems all too happy to break me back in. I certainly don't have the confidence I did as a teen, nor the inner thigh strength, but I know if I'm back for good, it's only a matter of time.

Like riding a bike. I shift uncomfortably in the saddle. *Only twice as painful.*

"You're right, Gypsy," I say to my red-brown Arabian. "Nevada does have the most beautiful sunrises." I miss the city but not the fog and tight packed buildings that obscure the morning sun. I lean forward and pat her shoulder. "And you are the perfect companion to share it with."

At this moment, I'm happy to be home.

Sure, I returned with my tail between my legs and just enough money to my name to start over. And yes, I'm even living with my parents—something I told myself I'd never do. It's a hit to the ego, but a temporary one.

"Trent would never have come out here with us," I explain to Gypsy, who continues her clop-stomping along the sandy trail. "He didn't even like the weekend visits. He preferred city comforts, like wine bars and clean sidewalks, to dusty trails."

Trent wouldn't come out on the trails with me if the world was ending. And yet I gave him five years. Five years of compromise and slow self-erasure.

I look back on what I 'lost' and wonder if it's not actually something I've gained.

I'd done my crying when the truth came out that our relationship was a farce. I'd gone through the depression, convinced my life was over. I even went through a bargaining phase where I actually thought I could talk my old life back into existence. Watching the sun as its fat yellow bottom clears the eastern hills, I feel a kind of peace I couldn't find back in the city—and for the first time in years, I feel content.

I'm ready to get back up on the horse (pun intended) and keep riding into a new future. With a few stipulations, of course, which I clarify to Gypsy.

"You know what I'm going to do, Gyps?" I muse. "I'm going to get that equine therapy certification and buy Carol's practice. I am going to have something that is real and solid and *mine*." Talking out loud helps. Even if she is, you know, a horse.

I pat her shoulder and shift in the saddle, the flannel shirt I threw on this morning already clinging where the sun's hit me. Beneath it, the tank I sleep in still smells faintly of last night's lavender lotion—at least it did when I set out.

"One thing's for sure," I add with conviction that pierces like the morning rays. "I am not—under *any* circumstances—getting myself into another damn situationship." I shift uncomfortably in my saddle. "Besides, I've got enough to worry about just with how much my ass hurts right now."

It's been, what—ten, twelve years since I've ridden more than a quick jaunt around my parent's property during a weekend visit. I recall Trent's complaints about his allergies. He never rode. Not once. He didn't like the animals on my dad's homestead, and to be honest, they didn't seem to care for him much either. He always made Gypsy particularly nervous. I shoulda known better.

I sigh. "You know what? You've got more sense than most people I know," I rub my hand down her mane. "And way better taste in men."

Gypsy snorts, clearly unimpressed with my flattery. And my taste in men.

"Come on, Gyps. Let's head back. I'm jonesing for my morning fix, and if I don't get off you soon, I won't walk right for a week." I pull on the lead to turn her around and give her belly a light squeeze with my calves.

I want a fresh start—but also a fresh latte. Healing doesn't mean going without foam. Gardnerville may be a small town but the only thing it has more of than ranches are cozy, comfortable coffee shops.

Since coming home, it's been home-brewed drip coffee, and my dad makes it thick as mud. Adding insult to injury, he's a black coffee kind of guy, so they have no creamer. While I'm sure he intends well, I'm not convinced that just 'adding a splash of milk' is enough to cut through the bitter sludge. So this morning, I'm treating myself to something that doesn't put so much hair on your chest. I'm thinking a lavender latte oughta do the trick.

My stomach gurgles. "And a pastry."

Gypsy huffs, not impressed.

"Don't worry, baby girl. I'll get you all fed and brushed down first." I run my hands down her neck as we meander our way back to the Wilkes Family Homestead.

It might take time, but I'll get my legs under me again. On the trail, and in life.

And step one: coffee that doesn't taste like regret.

Two

Sagebrush

Will

I stand on the stoop of the so-called ranch house, staring out at a sun-scorched wasteland of sagebrush, brittle weeds, and thorny ground cover that waits quietly, then clings like Velcro the second you step wrong. Massive wheel-line irrigation systems sit abandoned in the field—Chuck claims it used to grow alfalfa, but I'm not convinced anything's grown here since dial-up internet. Some of the wheels tilt at awkward angles, water pipes dangling like broken limbs. A few still stand, barely, the rusted connectors clinging like they know the end is near. Beside a white steel barn, another set lies in a heap, tangled with sun-bleached tumbleweeds and what might be the skeleton of a jackrabbit.

And that's just the outside.

The listing proudly described the inside as newly remodeled. Technically true. But that Pergo flooring trying to pass as wood didn't fool me for a second. The counter tops are quartzite. Functional, sure, but far from high-end.

I exhale slowly. This is a risky move, financially and practically. But for Gia, I'd take the gamble.

"So this is it?" I glance sideways at my little sister.

"Yes. Absolutely. One hundred percent, this is the one." Gia practically vibrates beside me, bouncing on her toes. "We've been over this. It's got everything we need to get started!"

"From the ground up, with all the risks that entails," I mutter under my breath.

She's only fourteen, but sometimes she strikes me as twice her age. Not right now. Right now, she's just a kid. A kid who lost her parents too soon and needs something—anything—to pour herself into. Most girls her age are into horseback riding lessons or art classes. Gia? She wants a ranch. A real, sweat-and-dirt-covered, acres-wide, horse riding bed and breakfast ranch. Agritourism. I don't even know where she learned that term.

"This is going to take a lot of fixing up if you want it to be operational," I warn, narrowing my eyes.

"Yep." She beams.

"And you're still going to school. Getting good grades." I say, mostly to hear myself say it.

"Yep."

She's been in online classes, already joining some local teen groups and making plans for community activities since winter break in preparation for our big move. With all the As she's been busting out, I don't actually have that leg to stand on.

I study her face, waiting—hoping—for a crack in her resolve. "Are you absolutely sure?"

Her grin only grows. "Do you remember working on Grandpa's farm?"

"Every summer until I went to college," I say, though the memory feels distant.

I let myself indulge in it for a second, but Grandpa's thriving Texas cattle operation has little in common with this rundown patch of high desert. His place was meticulous—every post mended, every line of fence straight. This property? The previous owners kept the buildings standing, but the land looks left for dead.

"It was so much fun!" Gia presses on. "I remember Grandpa telling me how

Sagebrush

he started with a single acre of weeds and turned it into a multimillion-dollar ranch with his bare hands. I want to do that."

I raise an eyebrow. "This property is a little more than an acre."

"Yeah, well, my vision is a little different," she says, propping her hands on her hips and staring out at the dry landscape that just officially became our home. "I need a good, solid location to build something that draws people in."

I sigh. Nevada. I thought the only things that draw people to Nevada are sex and gambling. And this sure felt like a gamble to me.

Still, it's not her money I'm gambling with—it's mine. Our inheritance was split between us after our parents passed but Gia can't touch hers for anything so risky until she turns eighteen.

Most of the Fitzgerald wealth came from Grandpa and is tangled in our family trust. It's still controlled by my Aunt Cathy, executive trustee and keeper of all things proper.

She made her feelings clear when I told her we were breaking grounds on a ranch in Nevada:

"It's a fools errand that can only end in a loss of investment."

What Dad left us came from *his* land, the vineyard project he broke off and built himself. A smaller, less political legacy. And it belongs to us, no strings attached.

Dad had the guts to stray from the family legacy and build something different. Maybe I owe Gia—and myself—the same kind of shot. Even if it feels like I'm walking into a dust bowl with a smile.

It's a long shot. But Gia's face is glowing with possibility.

"It's your money," I say again, softer this time. Investing in her venture was my idea, paying me back when she has access to her inheritance was hers.

As soon as the words leave my mouth, her excitement dims. Her hands drop. Shoulders slump. "You don't think it's a good idea, do you?"

No. I absolutely don't.

I spent years working with our grandfather. Gia remembers feeding goats and gathering eggs. I remember hauling hay, mucking stalls, and repairing fences in 110-degree heat. And it was nothing compared to what we have in store for us. This place isn't some hobby ranch. It's a fixer-upper with more sagebrush than soil.

But it doesn't matter what I think. When I look at her—at the light in her eyes—I pause. Ever since Mom and Dad died, she hasn't looked this alive. What matters is how much she needs this.

I put on a smile to hide my reservations. "Of course I do. I just want to make sure you do." I add a playful wink for good measure.

She explodes with joy, punching the air. "Yes! Yes, yes, yes!" She spins in a little victory circle, whooping.

I chuckle and hold out a hand. "Come on."

We walk across the gravel drive to a Lexus NX, where my friend and real estate agent, Chuck, is leaning up against the driver's side, busy on his phone. Chuck and I go way back. He's one of the few people from college I still talk to. When Gia came to me with this wild idea of building a ranch empire from scratch, I knew exactly who to call.

Chuck is crisp and clean despite the dusty landscape: white button up, blue blazer, and a neatly trimmed red beard framing a wide smile—the guy hasn't changed a bit since college.

As we approach, he cocks his head to the side and somehow, his smile manages to grow.

"Ah, Beth!"

His fingers tap away at the screen.

I quirk a brow. "Ooooh. Beth. I didn't know you were seeing someone."

Chuck waves me off, nervously. "Oh, no, no. Nothing like that. Prospective client." He struggles to tuck his phone into his back pocket. "So—what do you think?"

I look over at Gia. "I'd say we're ready to start tearing up the land and turning it into a proper investment!" I extend a hand. "Thanks for all your work on this, man!"

Chuck skips the handshake and goes for a full-on hug. He's one of two men allowed to hug me like that. The other was my dad. I give the thought just a second, then push it aside. Chuck gives my back a hearty pat, just what

Sagebrush

I need to bring me back to the present.

"Anything for you, bro," he says with genuine warmth. "You ready for the next step?"

I let out a long breath and turn, waving my arms out wide to indicate all the work ahead of us. "I mean…"

"Yes!" Gia elbows me harder than strictly necessary. "Yes, we are!"

Chuck raises an eyebrow. "Well, if you decide you need some help, I know a guy. Actually, he's the one I just mentioned. He's great on a ranch and the smartest mother fu—" he looks at Gia, "I mean, smartest guy I know. I'm sure he'd be happy to consult at the very least."

"I'll be sure to hit you up when I get sick of clearing weeds." I wink at Gia.

She is so confident that won't happen, it's practically oozing out of her. I give her a week.

"Absolutely, bro. I'll be sure to let you know. Not that we'll need it." Actually, we need to hire an entire construction company to raze the place and rebuild it—but who am I to say it?

"Welp." Chuck claps his hands together. "I'd love to help you get settled in, but I've got an appointment with a client in just shy of an hour."

"Ooooh!" Gia puts her hands to her lips. "Is it Beth?" She draws out the name.

Chuck laughs and shakes his head, cheeks flushing. "You're both awful. And no. It's just another client, a family from Reno looking to get out of the Biggest Little City."

I scoff inwardly. Leaving the city to come out here… on purpose? Then the irony of the thought hits me and I stifle a cough.

"Hey," I throw out as Chuck moves to open the driver's side door. "You know a place where I could grab a cup of coffee? We got in late last night and all I've had to eat this morning is a package of Gia's Poptarts."

Chuck chuckles. "I know just the place." He taps on his phone and within a few seconds, I hear the beep of the incoming message. Before I can thank him, he exclaims, "Oh! I almost forgot!"

He pops open the rear passenger door. "I got you both a little something, like a welcome home gift." He says with his head tucked into the back seat.

He pulls out two shiny cowboy hats. The larger one is a crisp cream—plain, simple, and formal. The other is a dusty brown wicker with a leather band adorned with silver and turquoise pendants.

I smile despite myself. "Gee, Chuck. Thanks." I try to sound genuine.

"I got them to go with these." He holds up an envelope. "Concert tickets. Your real closing gift is still a few weeks out, but I wanted you to have something on your first day here."

"A concert? In Gardnerville?" I'm skeptical.

"You'd be surprised," Chuck says with a smirk.

Gia already has hers on and looks cute as a button. Like she already belongs here.

"Try yours on!" she insists.

So I do.

I thank Chuck and add, "Maybe this will help me blend in with the locals."

I hand the envelope to Gia. I'm not exactly dying to mingle, but she clutches that envelope like it contains Taylor Swift tickets and a backstage pass.

"Well, Booger, you coming with me to this…" I pull out my phone and scan Chuck's text. "DST place?"

"Hard pass. I've logged enough hours in that beast," she says, nodding at the truck. "Just bring me back something delicious!"

Chuck hops into his SUV and pulls away. I climb into my new Silverado—still rocking the dealer placard and that fresh-off-the-lot smell. And, of course, I've still got the ridiculous cowboy hat on.

As I glance back at the property, I try to see it the way Gia does. Not sagebrush and sun-scorched fences—but possibility.

I tip the hat at my reflection in the rear view mirror. "That's right, Will. New ranch. New hat. New you."

If only I didn't miss the old me so much.

Three

Meet Cute

Will

The coffee shop is only a few minutes down the road. The outside is blue and decorated with Nevada imagery. I step inside, and I'm hit with a blend of modern, clean aesthetics and small-town charm. Best of all, I smell the grounds. Smooth, roasted coffee beans, not bitter or burned.

My stomach growls again as I step into line. The menu is blessedly simple—no fourteen-step coffee orders here. I like trying a new and exotic drink, but the lavender latte seems a bit too earthy for my tastes. I think this morning I'll play it safe with a mocha.

I cross my arms and lean slightly out of line to glimpse at the pastry case. It's mid-morning so the pickings are slim, but I see a couple of muffins and what looks like some cookies.

And then the doorbell rattles.

"Welcome in!" the barista calls, then returns their attention to the customer at the counter.

"Thanks!" comes a sweet, feminine voice behind me.

I turn and there she is.

The cutest thing I've ever seen.

Messy brown curls are piled into one of those cloth headbands, strands escaping in every direction. A faded green-and-black flannel hangs off one shoulder, the strap of her canvas bag slipping like it's a second from falling off completely. Underneath, she wears a white cropped tank and real jeans—worn from use, not trend.

She tugs the flannel back onto her shoulder with a sigh and adjusts a pair of thin-rimmed glasses on a lightly freckled nose. Her skin is sunkissed—just enough to suggest she spends time outside, but not enough to mark her as one of the leathery lifers who work under the sun all day.

The look is effortless, in the sense that I can tell she put no effort into it. She is unpolished, uncoordinated, and absolutely captivating.

She is so far from my usual type. I have refined taste; I prefer the polish. I am all for a woman who is intentional and put-together. Classy, I think is the word. But something about her raw, unaffected energy—her strength, her casual confidence in not caring—hits me square in the chest.

She finally gets herself figured out and looks up at me. She catches my gaze, and the smile that bursts onto her face is wide, exuberant, and entirely unfiltered.

* * *

Beth

"Oooh, would you look at that! A real cowboy!" The words leave my mouth before my inner monologue can tackle them to the ground.

"What? Where?" The man glances around in mock confusion before lowering his voice conspiratorially. "You know, when I first got here, I didn't even think Nevada had ranches."

I gasp, "You didn't?"

That's when I really took him in.

Tall. Fit. A stunning jawline, way too clean shaven for any pragmatic ranch worker. Brand new tan straw hat revealing just a trace of gray peppered through the dark hair at his temples. He looks like he just walked out of a fashion magazine that is part GQ part Modern Cowboy. His deep brown eyes sparkle with the joke we're sharing.

My gaze drifts lower. Crisp black button-up. Jeans that have never met a patch of dirt. Hey, I may be off the market, but that doesn't mean I can't window shop.

He's too polished to be a working ranch hand. If he's ever used a post hole digger, it probably came with instructions. Still, something about the way he owns the look makes me pause.

He puts a perfectly manicured hand to his chest. "I didn't. I thought Nevada was all about gambling and sex."

"New in town?" I wager.

City Slicker spreads his arms. "How can you tell?"

I tilt my head, feigning analysis. "Hmmm…Let's see. The hat is too new. The jeans, too crisp. And that shirt?" I scoff. "Maybe for a night out, but one second on a ranch, and that thing will melt off in horror. What is that, silk?"

His lips parted in mock offense. "Cotton. It's Brioni."

I have no idea what that means, but I'm on a roll. "Let me guess—that's your Silverado outside?"

His eyes gleam. "Damn, you're good."

We step forward in line.

I cross my arms and size him up. "Eh, it doesn't take a rocket scientist." I find myself smiling in spite of myself.

"Fair enough." His grin is so charming I almost forget why I came in here. "So what's wrong with my look? The hat? It's the hat isn't it?"

I can't tell if he's joking or sincerely seeking feedback, but I throw him a bone.

I nod, giving him my best cringe smile. "It won't last two seconds out in the weather."

He laughs and pulls it off his head. Perfectly sculpted close-cropped hair underneath.

Because why not?

The espresso machine hisses as the barista passes a steaming cup across the counter as we advance forward. We're almost up. I'm not sure if I'm anxious to get my coffee or hoping the line moves slower so I can keep digging myself deeper.

He turns it over, considering it. "My friend gave it to me this morning."

"Well, that explains a lot." I take it from him and twirl it in my hands.

"Too much?" He inquires.

I check the inside. Tag's still there—$145. My eyebrows shoot up.

That's a nice friend you've got there, City Slicker.

"Not at all," I shrug as I position it on my head. "It's perfect for a night out. Something like dancing or a country concert."

I don't know why but that makes him laugh.

I strike a pose, "How do I look?"

"Gorgeous," he says, and it's not flirty—it's breathless.

Damnit. I actually blush. I look down and curtsey, a playful move that gives me time to calm the nerves dancing through my body.

"So what brings someone like you to the valley?" I ask casually. Not that I care.

"I've got a project in the works at one of the ranches." His answer is cryptic, but also, like, duh, of course you do. So I remain silent until he adds, "Fitzgerald Ranch."

I frown. "Fitzgerald? Haven't heard of it."

"Newly purchased. I think it used to be called Silver Pine, Silver Brush..."

I nearly drop my bag. "Silver Sage Ranch?"

He nods. "That's the one! The land's been undeveloped for years, but we're bringing it back to life."

I snort. "I heard someone bought it. Didn't realize they'd renamed it."

His eyes widen and I see mischief behind them. "You didn't?"

"Newp." I shake my head. "The place had history. Shame, really." I remember the fall harvest carnival where I helped at the cotton candy booth as a teen.

"I'd say the real shame is the state it's sitting in now."

Poetic. Okay, maybe the man knows how to look on the bright side.

"True," I admit, then add, "But come on—'Fitzgerald Ranch'? That's not about honoring local history. That's legacy branding. Total ego move."

Something shifts in his face—just a second of tension. A flicker of something I can't quite place. I almost think he's angry.

I mean, I *did* just insult his boss.

Then the smile returns, easy and wide, as though I imagined the shift.

"Who knows." He says with a shrug. "Maybe it'll have history again."

I don't bother arguing, but with a name like that? I'm not hopeful..

"And you have worked on a ranch before?" I ask, lifting a brow.

He scratches the back of his neck, suddenly sheepish. "I have. A long time ago. Summers with my grandfather. Then I did a stint in the corporate world. All desks and contracts."

The words are out before I can stop them. "Looks like you could hold your own, though."

I regret it instantly.

And I'm still wearing his hat. I take it off, give it one more nonchalant spin in my hands, and hand it back with a wink.

Damnit, Beth, cool it with the moves!

"I'm Beth by the way," I add casually. I suppose it's a bit too late for handshakes, but I extend my hand anyway.

He hesitates- just for a second- then clears his throat.

"Name's Bill." His grip is firm, his hand soft, uncalloused. "Nice to meet you."

City Slicker Bill steps up to place his order, then turns to me. "You wanna chat over a cup of coffee? Being new here and all, I'd love the chance to chat with one of the locals."

Were he an older gentleman looking for friendly conversation? Sure. A woman with a book I'd read? Absolutely. But a dangerously attractive ranch noob?

The answer is clearly no.

So of course, like a fool, I smile. "Sure, that sounds nice."

A few minutes later, I stare at my untouched e-reader as my coffee steams between my hands. His hat is sitting on the table between us, now the object that holds our brief shared history in its woven strands.

This is not how I had planned my morning. I came here to drink coffee and read in peace—not get tangled up in cowboy-flavored distraction.

Across from me, City Slicker- because I still don't know the guy's name- leans back in his chair, looking way too comfortable in his city-boy cowboy fusion.

"So, horse therapy?" He taps a finger against his mug. "You're going to provide therapy… to horses?"

I laugh a beat too long at his joke. Am I seriously crushing on a man whose hat still has the price tag on it?

"No," I say with a small laugh. "I'm going to provide therapy for people, using horses. Equine-assisted therapy."

His expression stays blank for a beat. Then his mouth quirks into something almost playful.

"So, you're saying horses aren't the clients?"

"You joke, but I bet they'd have a lot to say about their humans." I give him a wink, then immediately want to slap myself.

Subtle, Beth. Real subtle.

His laugh is soft this time, almost thoughtful.

For a brief moment, something about this feels…easy. Familiar. Like we aren't two strangers who just met.

He lifts his mug, eyes warm over the rim as he takes a slow sip. "Tell me more," he says, like we've got all the time in the world. And somehow, against all logic, I do.

Four

Vision

Will

When I get home, Gia is sprawled on the couch with her laptop balanced on her legs, stylus in one hand, tapping away. Her eyes are laser-focused. She doesn't even look up when I walk in.

I toss the blueberry muffin across the room.

She catches it one-handed. "Thanks!" she chirps, already peeling the wrapper. "Took you long enough."

I drop my keys on the table and collapse into the armchair across from her. "Got caught up talking to someone local."

I don't tell her I almost forgot the muffin completely because I was too busy playing verbal tennis with a woman who is all contradictions—sarcasm and softness, guarded and somehow glowing. The kind of woman who seems like she'd either heal you or slap you with a saddle pad. I can't decide which I'd prefer. I also leave out that I circled back into the coffee shop because I'd left in such a daze, I forgot to grab it the first time. The point is, I brought the muffin.

"Did you at least get anything useful out of it?" Gia asks between bites.

I hesitate. Beth's face flashes in my head—piercing eyes, unapologetic confidence, the way she took one look at my designer ranch getup and saw right through itl.

"I learned that horse therapy is a real thing."

Gia lights up immediately. "What, like therapy *with* horses?"

"Apparently. The woman—Beth—she's a therapist. Uses horses to help people or something like that."

Gia props her elbow on the arm of the couch, the muffin held aloft like a trophy. "That is actually so cool. Can we go meet her horses?"

"She didn't exactly offer an open invitation," I say. "Besides, we've got our own mess to figure out."

Gia rolls her eyes and flips the laptop screen around. "Speaking of which, look what I came up with."

The screen is filled with a colorful schematic. I have no idea how she made it—it's part digital sketch, part cartography, and part fever dream. She launches into an explanation without waiting for my brain to catch up.

"I walked the property while you were gone. It took forever. I stepped in, like, eight sticker bushes and saw a rabbit the size of a corgi. But it's got *so* much potential. Like over here?" She points to a blob that might be a rectangle. "Guest cabins. And here—trails. And I figured we can do a gazebo or pergola or something artsy for weddings. Oh! And maybe a little zen garden with desert plants and benches."

She barely pauses to breathe between bites of muffin.

I lean forward, squinting at the plans. "Didn't realize you had all this rattling around in your head."

"I've been talking it through with some friends on Discord," she says, brushing a crumb off her hoodie. "Tessa and Malik are obsessed. They want to come out once the cabins are built and help with the garden. And I started messaging with this local youth group—they do community cleanup projects and local volunteering. I might help with their next horse rescue event."

She says it so casually, like she's not building a whole new life from scratch.

I study her for a second. Fourteen. Still just a kid in a thousand ways, but she's laying groundwork with more confidence than most adults I know. Meanwhile, I'm still trying to figure out what size hinge we need for the back gate.

I let out a breath and nod toward the laptop. "Come on. Let's walk the property. You can show me where all this magic is supposed to happen."

Her face lights up.

Two hours and one tour later, my boots are covered in dust, and I've got a vague but functional understanding of Gia's plan. She wants goats, chickens, horses, cabins, a fire pit, maybe even a corn maze or pumpkin patch by fall. The garden will be built to accommodate kids and guests. The place is going to be family-friendly and Instagram-worthy if she has anything to say about it.

"This property's a mess," I say honestly as we stop near the barn.

"I know." She lifts her chin like she's daring me to challenge her.

"But your vision? It's solid and clear, kiddo. Better than some of my project managers," I admit.

She tries to hide her smile, but it creeps across her face anyway.

"What do you think?" she asks, watching me with a mixture of pride and nerves.

I scan the land again. The fixer-upper isn't just the ranch—it's both of us. Gia rebuilding her sense of belonging. Me trying to make peace with this stripped-down version of life.

"I think," I say, "we've got our work cut out for us. But if this is your dream, I'm all in."

"Sick!" She shouts, pumping a fist in the air. "We're really gonna do this!"

"Sure," I say, more to myself than to her. "How hard can it be?"

Five

Grit and Determination

Beth

"She's coming along nicely," Carol says, her practiced eyes scanning Gypsy as I lead her through slow, deliberate circles near the fence line.

We're sticking to ground work today—treats, voice cues, body language. After the ride I put in this morning, my legs are still pissed. There's a bruise blooming on my inner thigh and I swear I pulled a butt muscle.

"She's smart and patient," I say, giving Gypsy a scratch behind the ears. "But she's too independent for beginners." I hesitate.

Carol hands me the lead with a smirk. "Sounds familiar."

I snort. "Yeah, yeah."

We work in tandem, her consulting a checklist while I lead Gypsy in another lap. I try to keep my mind on the job—on the horses, the future of this business, the way my breath slows when I'm around animals again—but it drifts.

Not toward anything helpful. Not toward progress notes or business plans. Nope. Toward the infuriating, confusing, too-handsome-for-his-own-good stranger from the coffee shop.

Dammit.

"Earth to Bethany," Carol calls from the other side of the pen.

I blink. "Sorry. Lost in thought."

"I noticed," she says, amused. "Your head's been in the clouds ever since you got back from town."

"It's not like that." I wave her off. "I just… ran into someone. Briefly."

"Mmhmm."

I shoot her a look. "I'm not interested."

"Sure." She grins. "What's his name?"

"Bill." I grimace. "Don't say it."

Carol laughs. "I wasn't gonna."

"I don't even know why I gave him my number. He probably thinks he's God's gift to Gardnerville."

"Is he?" she asks lightly.

"Maybe. If God was in the business of designer flannel and perfect hair." I rub Gypsy's neck a little harder than necessary. "Guys like that are always too good to be true."

Carol doesn't answer. She doesn't need to. The silence says it all.

"I'm not looking," I say, quieter this time. "Last time I let myself fall for someone charming and polished, I ended up broke, humiliated, and paying for a storage unit I never even opened."

Carol finally looks over. "You're allowed to be curious without giving him your whole heart, you know."

"Yeah. Well. Right now, I'd rather give all that to this girl right here." I pat Gypsy's neck.

"Fair enough."

Gypsy shifts beside me, her ears flicking back to catch the sound of our conversation. Her posture is relaxed, her gaze soft. She's not as jumpy as she used to be, but she still doesn't warm up to just anyone. I'm pretty sure she likes Ben more than she likes me, despite being my horse. Could be the years of absence weren't lost on her.

Carol watches her for a beat. "You keep working with her like this? She might actually be ready when you take over."

I nod. "It's what I'm hoping."

I don't say the rest aloud. That I *need* her to be ready. That I need to prove to myself that I'm not just playing equine therapist in borrowed boots. That this version of my life—horses, hay, muddy boots, early mornings—has to stick. Because I'm not going back to cardigans and city smog and empty apartments.

We make another slow lap, Gypsy stopping perfectly when I breathe out and drop my hand. She's picking up on my cues. That's something.

My dad, Ben, appears from the side yard, his flannel rolled to the elbows and a grease smear on one cheek. "How's it feel?" he asks as he walks toward us.

I chuckle. "Like I'm walking around with sore muscles I forgot existed."

"You know what that means, right?" He raises a brow.

"That I need to ride more."

"That your ass is gonna hurt later."

"Thanks, Dad," I sigh. "But you're wrong. It already does."

All three of us laugh. The sound feels good. Easy.

For a second, I let myself remember that I used to be this girl—ranch dust on her boots, sweat on her brow, cracking jokes with her dad like it was the most natural thing in the world. But somewhere between high school and heartbreak, I traded her for someone else.

Now, maybe, she's clawing her way back.

Ben claps me on the shoulder and reaches for Gypsy's lead. "You've still got it. Just need to dust it off."

I smile, but there's something bittersweet behind it. I might still have "it"—but "it" is all shriveled and neglected. Rebuilding muscles, habits, and lifestyle...well, it's like I tell my clients: it takes time.

We stand for a beat, the three of us watching the desert sunset stretch out in wild swaths of coral and purple. Carol whistles low. "Every time I think I've seen it all, this sky pulls out a new trick."

"Steals the show," I say softly.

My dad wraps an arm around me. "Took you long enough to drag your sorry hide back home."

"Sorry and sore," I admit. "But I'm here."

He squeezes my shoulder, the way only he can. "Wouldn't have it any other way."

Carol says her goodbyes and disappears inside to chat up her best friend Missy, who I call Mom. Dad and I walk Gypsy back to the stalls he built with his own hands—solid, sturdy, no nonsense. Just like him.

I look at the rows of fencing, the new barn- with a door that still needs oiling, and all the rest of the work Dad put into making this land his. This life isn't sleek. It isn't glossy. It's muddy, raw, real. It takes grit and determination.

And it's mine. Or it will be. Eventually.

Six

Offbeat

Beth

The opening act is a local up-and-coming band that blends country with rock and rap. I have to admit, they're pretty decent, but talking over them—even way back at the beer stands—is a chore. One I perform most enthusiastically.

"I heard the new owner of Silver Sage is just another rich guy playing cowboy," I say, sipping my beer. "Probably bought the place for the aesthetic."

Jane rolls her eyes. "Beth."

"What?" I shrug. "It's true. Just another wealthy outsider who might not appreciate the ranch's local history. Bet he doesn't even know the difference between alfalfa and cheatgrass."

Chuck coughs into his drink. I barely notice.

"Beth," Jane says again, her tone shifting.

Even Carol is looking at me in a way I can't quite read, but I'm already in it, so I double down.

I wave her off. "I mean, no offense to him personally. But William Fitzgerald—sounds fancy, but maybe he's just misunderstood."

"Yeah, about that—" Chuck starts.

I turn, mid-rant, beer in hand—and lock eyes with Bill.

My stomach flutters. Heat floods my neck. Cowboy hat. Smirk. Gorgeous.

Chuck grins. "Beth, allow me to introduce Will, the gentleman who owns Fitzgerald Ranch."

His arms are crossed like he's been standing there long enough to hear every word.

"Alas, it was the name my parents bestowed upon me." He uncrosses his arms and shrugs, gaze skimming the crowd like he's searching for his escape route.

Delightful butterflies turn toxic in my stomach as two realizations hit me simultaneously. First, Bill, the sexy city boy playing ranch hand, was William Fitzgerald—the billionaire bringing a "vision" to Silver Sage. And second, he likely just heard everything I said.

I scramble to save face, forcing a tight smile. "So, you're Will," I say, voice steadier than I feel.

He nods once, all formality, and takes my hand in a polite, cool handshake. The warmth from the coffee shop is gone.

"Nice to see you again, Beth."

I nod, trying to stay composed. "Likewise."

My mind's racing, but my face—God, I hope my face is calm. He must think I'm a joke. Some judgmental small-town girl. The fake smile's starting to ache.

Carol jumps in like a lifeline tossed from a boat. "Oh look! There's George and his wife. You kids have fun!" She disappears into the crowd with practiced grace.

Chuck hands Will a beer, then gestures between us. "You two know each other?"

"We've met," Will says, finally looking at me with something like amusement.

I return it with a shrug. "Briefly. At a coffee shop."

His mouth twitches. He's enjoying this too much.

My cheeks burn, but I refuse to let it show. So I do what any reasonable, cornered woman would do. I smile bigger.

"I'm sorry," I say. "I just… I'm not sure what to say."

Chuck raises a brow, curious, but thankfully doesn't press. Jane does me the favor of pulling focus.

"Chuck, you wanna come dance?" she asks sweetly.

Chuck glances at Will, then back to her. "Yeah, sure. I'll give it a shot. Will?"

"I'll pass. Not a dancer." He looks at me when he says it, deliberate and cool.

I bite back a snort. "Neither am I. Come on, Jane, let's go make fools of ourselves."

As I tug Jane toward the crowd, I hear him mutter, "Too late."

My spine straightens, but I keep walking.

We dance. We laugh. We drink. At least, on the surface. Underneath, I'm spiraling. Every time I try to let it go, my thoughts boomerang back to him. To what I said. To the easy way we connected at the coffee shop.

I don't even know who he really is.

At some point, Chuck and Jane vanish into the dance crowd, and I find myself alone. I wander the edges of the amphitheater, scanning the beer tents and merchandise booths, just trying to breathe.

That's when I see him—back to me, phone pressed to his ear.

"Hi, Gigi!" he says brightly, voice warm. "Where have you been?"

My body stills. I take cover behind the end of a vendor's tent. Eavesdropping is bad. I know that. I also don't move.

"Sure honey. Yeah, whatever you like. Look, use the card I gave you, but be careful—it has a five-hundred-dollar spending limit. I doubt you'll need more than that, but call me if you do... Okay. Have fun. Love you too."

He pockets the phone.

Girlfriend. Of course. Probably someone beautiful and brilliant who wouldn't be caught dead misjudging him in public. Gigi. Ugh. Even her name sounds intimidating.

Chuck walks up behind him and claps him on the shoulder. "Will! There you are. Having fun?"

"Sure. Gia's having herself a blast, and I'm over here worrying."

I frown. *Gia?*

"She'll be fine. These are good people," Chuck reassures.

Then Chuck says the one thing I don't want to hear.

"What do you think of the Wilkes sisters?"

My breath catches.

"Yes, I saw you dancing with Jane. Lovely lady," Will says evenly.

Chuck chuckles nervously. "What about Beth? She's quite a gal, isn't she?"

"Honestly?" Will sighs. "What's that expression? Not exactly my type?"

My heart sinks.

Not my type.

I stand frozen for a few seconds before slipping away into the crowd, shame and anger threading through me like barbed wire. I feel stupid. Exposed.

I wander back toward the main crowd and spot my parents. Their laughter feels like it's coming from a world I'm no longer part of.

Mom notices me instantly.

"Honey, what's wrong?"

"I think the alcohol's catching up to me," I lie.

She nods toward my dad. "Ben, get Bethie a water, will you?"

I don't even argue. When Carol's arm drops over my shoulder, I lean into her without thinking.

"That was a right shit show earlier," she mutters. "How'd it go?"

"You mean after you bailed?" I tease.

"Some things you youngsters gotta face on your own," she shrugs.

Jane joins us, eyes searching mine. "Beth, how did you not know?"

"He said his name was Bill," I say flatly. "He seemed…not rich." And sweet. And maybe a little lost. A man trying to find his footing, like me. But no. That was just a fantasy.

"Girl, don't you read the paper?" Carol hands me her beer.

"The paper?" I take a swig.

"His face was plastered on the front page," Jane adds. "When he closed on the ranch."

I take another gulp and hand the beer back. "Guess I dodged a bullet."

Jane laughs softly. "How so?"

"I was actually starting to like Bill. The last thing I need is a complication.

Good thing my mouth got in the way."

Carol raises her beer. "To knowing when to walk."

Mom swaps my beer for water. "And to knowing when not to stay."

I smile weakly. "Thanks, Mom."

She winks. "Sexy's easy to find. Character's the trick."

The first chords of Aaron Lewis pulse through the speakers. I raise my cup.

"To uncomplicated nights and country music," I declare, but under the toast and the bravado is that quiet ache. The one that says maybe I got it wrong. Again.

The crowd cheers. The lights blur. And somewhere deep in my chest, something curls up small and bruised.

Seven

Un-Phased

Beth

An hour later, I'm full of meatloaf, sprawled out on the couch next to Jane as Dad spreads his run of seven out on the card table in front of us. Phase 10 is well in progress, a familiar warmth spreading through me as laughter fills the room—or at least, it was, until half of us got distracted by wine and the other half started arguing about whether we're actually following the rules.

I think that's how Ben Wilkes wins. Divide and conquer. Only he does it by sitting back and playing quietly as we women fall right into the trap and do all the hard work ourselves.

For instance:

"Alright," Mom says, with the kind of casual cheer that means she's about to emotionally body-slam us. "When are one of you girls going to settle down and give me some grandbabies?"

Dad snorts from across the table as we get our last chances to go out. His cocked smile and head shake says it all, "Nope. Not getting involved in this one."

Jane pretends to be fascinated by her hand. "Mom."

"What?" Mom blinks innocently, perched on the edge of her seat with a glass of boxed wine like it's a communion chalice. "I'm just wondering if my womb will ever see justice."

"I'm sorry, your what?" I almost spit-take my wine.

She waves a hand dramatically. "My womb! My *legacy*! Two smart, beautiful daughters and not a single baby to show for it."

"This month's romance book club is succubus themed," I say flatly. "Pretty sure I'm not anyone's idea of maternal right now."

"You're just in a phase," she says, dismissing me with a sip. "You'll get through it. And you," she turns on Jane, "aren't you still seeing that one guy? What's his name, the clarinet player?"

"That was two years ago, Mom."

"Well, he seemed nice."

"He cried because I ate the last pickle."

"Well, *I* like men who show their emotions," Mom huffs. "And who don't let good food go to waste."

"Jesus," Dad mutters, half-laughing. "You girls are feral."

"We were raised by wolves," I say, fanning out my cards like a fan of knives and winking at them both.

"Damn right," Dad chuckles. "And now look at you—untamable."

"I'm focusing on my career," Jane says sweetly, glancing at me as backup arrives. "But I mean, if the right guy came along…"

Missy perks up like a hawk spotting a rodent. "See! That's all I'm saying. Keep your hearts open. And your legs. For God's sake, your biological clocks are ticking!"

"Mom!" we both groan in unison.

She grins, totally unbothered. "Just saying. I had both of you before I was thirty."

"Yeah," I say dryly. "And you also used lead-based paint and let us lick envelopes unsupervised."

"Better immune systems for it," Dad quips.

"Times change," I say, grabbing a cracker from the snack plate. "First you get the money, then the crotch goblins."

"Beth Wilkes!" Mom gasps.

"What? You were the one who just told us to go have sex!" I defend, chasing my cracker with a swig of red wine.

Jane chokes on her drink, and Dad smirks without shame.

"You're a doctor," Mom scolds. "You make plenty."

The words land with a quiet thud. My fingers freeze mid-cracker.

"Sucker punch," Jane murmurs behind her fanned out cards.

Mom sighs and reaches across the table. "I'm sorry, honey. That was… that wasn't fair. You're doing your best."

I take a slow breath and soften. "I'm starting over. That takes time."

"And maybe a puppy," Dad adds helpfully. "Less paperwork."

Mom shoots him a look. Apparently a dog is *not* the kind of grandbaby she is looking for.

"If I have kids, I'm probably just adopting anyway," Jane says airily. "Less drama."

"That's my girl," Dad says.

We're finally settling back in when the front door opens.

"Sorry I'm late! Got caught up on a contract."

A bottle of wine appears, followed by Chuck Miller—broad-shouldered, glasses fogging, the energy of a man unsure if he's entering a party or an ambush.

"Chuck!" Mom calls like he's a long-lost relative. "Girls, I forgot to tell you! Chuck's joining us tonight."

The name hits me like a cold splash of water. Chuck. As in Will's friend. As in concert-enabler. As in—

*No. No, no, no. We are **not** thinking about Bill right now.*

Chuck waves cheerfully, easily blending into our close-knit family dynamic, setting the wine down. "Pleasure to finally meet you all in person."

He's cute in that charming golden retriever way. Curly hair. Trim beard. Strong but unassuming. The kind of guy you'd trust to help you move your couch and not ghost you afterward.

"Nice to meet you," I say, shaking his hand. "Thanks for bringing fresh booze!"

"Happy to." He looks around like he's walked into a sitcom. "Y'all are…

lively."

"That's one word for it," Jane says.

Mom ushers him in like an honored guest. Dad pats the seat next to him. "Safe zone's over here."

Chuck eases into the chair like he's found a bunker.

"So," Dad says, dealing cards. "How's real estate?"

"Busy. Picked up a new contract today." Chuck sets his glass down. "Oh, and Ben—I passed your info to my buddy Will. Said he might need a consult on fencing."

My hand stills mid-deal.

Will. Not Bill. Not coffee shop flirtation turned mild trainwreck. No, this is real ranch project, concert-attending, finger-licking, mysterious-as-hell Will.

I force a casual sip of wine but I can feel the flush rising in my cheeks.

Ben brightens. "Will, huh? Sure thing. I like helping out where I can."

I consider the ramifications. Will needs help, huh? Maybe he got in over his head. I want to focus on that- perhaps even revel in it, but instead I think about the concert and a mixed bag of feelings hits all at once.

...Was I *mean*?

...Was he *playing me*?

...Do even I care?

My mouth tastes bitter, so I rinse it down with another drink, a decent swig this time.

"Beth?" Jane elbows me.

I blink. "What?"

"You in for Sheriff of Nottingham?"

"Always." I cough.

Chuck laughs nervously. "Uh oh. The look on your faces. Should I be scared?"

"Oh, you'll love it," Jane says. "This game is all lying and smuggling."

Chuck glances at me. "I thought you were a therapist."

"I am." I smile. "But I moonlight as a con artist." I feel the swill in my mind begin to dissipate.

Chuck laughs, looking vaguely terrified and weirdly charmed, exactly what I expect. We Wilkes' have a way about us that requires a certain palette.

Dad sets up the game as Jane and I mock fight over pieces we don't really care about. Mom pours Chuck more wine as he chuckles at us and blushes, his eyes always wandering back to Jane. The evening proceeds comfortably and it seems as if Dad's real estate buddy fits right in.

Still not my type. But dammit, he held his own.

Eight

Catching Crushes

Beth

"What'd you think about Chuck?" Jane asks casually.

Game night is over and Chuck is gone. I'm helping her set up the second guest room so she can crash here. She only lives fifteen minutes away, but the boxed wine flowed freely and Jane is a lightweight. Chuck might've been clear-headed enough to drive, but Jane? Not a chance.

"I think the more important question is 'what do you think?'" I toss her a look as I straighten the edge of the fitted sheet. She's not slick. I saw the heart eyes during Taboo.

"I think he's really sweet." She smiles, and I don't miss the slight blush on her cheeks. "And kinda handsome, you know? In a cute, unconventional way." She lifts her side of the mattress and eyes me over it. "Now, your turn."

"I think he's great," I say, keeping it breezy. "Not my type, but definitely a decent human. And I could tell you two hit it off tonight." Just because I'm not looking doesn't mean I can't be thrilled for my sister.

"You're not into him because you're still thinking about coffee shop man," she singsongs.

"Am not." It comes out like a petulant five-year-old.

Jane smirks. "Uh-huh. That's why all night it was 'Will said this,' and 'Can you believe he's turning Silver Sage into a tourist trap?'" She tosses me the other end of the fitted sheet like it's Exhibit A.

Big sisters are the worst.

"Give me a break," I mutter. "He's the first real conversation I've had outside the family since I got back." I smooth out the wrinkles a little too aggressively. Even I don't buy the bullshit I'm selling.

"What about Carol?" Jane doesn't let up.

"She's practically our aunt," I say. "Doesn't count."

"Convenient technicality."

I sigh, grabbing the flat sheet. "Well, even so, I've got my plan. And that plan does not include men."

"At all?"

"Right now," I emphasize. "Right now it doesn't." I pause, folding the sheet carefully. "Every time I think I like someone, it turns out I'm just attracted to the exact wrong kind of person. I don't trust my instincts anymore."

Jane quiets.

"Honestly," I add, softer now, "I think I'm better off rebuilding myself before I try to figure anyone else out. Maybe some people just aren't wired for this stuff."

Her voice is gentle when she says, "Or maybe some people just haven't met the right electrician yet."

I laugh, despite myself. "Cute."

She shrugs. "I'm just saying... you light up when you talk about him. Whether you want to or not."

I wave her off. "Let's talk about you and Chuck."

And oh, boy, does that work.

"Did you see the way he plays Taboo?" she gushes. "Unassuming but *so* smart! And that smile? I mean—"

"He's so shy and geeky," I tease.

Jane throws a pillow at me.

"Maybe shy and geeky is exactly what I need."

"I think you just need to get laid." I chuck the pillow back.

"Beth!" she squeals, then sighs. "Maybe you're right."

She flops onto the half-made bed, limbs everywhere, smiling up at the ceiling like a teenager in love.

I fall down next to her and lace my fingers through hers. "Of course I'm not right. You are sweet and shy, he's sweet and shy. Match made in small-town heaven."

She giggles, tucking her cheek against her shoulder. "Dad's been talking about them working on some investments together. He said Chuck went to some Ivy League school. Can you imagine?"

I whistle. "Pragmatic *and* cute. Jackpot."

"Am I dumb for feeling this giddy about him? I just met the guy."

I think about the man with the too-handsome smile, the surprising depth, and the way my stomach keeps tying itself in knots over him. At least Jane's crush has a clean origin story.

"Not dumb," I say finally. "I think your heart's exactly where it's supposed to be."

Nine

Just a Fence

Will

Gia and I drive down the highway in my truck, which is loaded with lumber to fix one of the horse corrals. Home Depot is half an hour away, which by city standards means pretty close. By rural standards, it's a whole town over. The road is one long stretch of four lane highway through cow field after nauseating cow field. The flow of traffic is interrupted by several stop lights... on a highway. I grumble as the flashing lights hanging above the highway indicate that I need to go from 65 to nada as one of the lights turn red.

I look over as I slow the truck to a stop. Gia is next to me, her head bopping away to a tune playing in her earbuds. She grabs her bright pink Jamba Juice and takes a sip as her eyes wander out the window. She's happy as can be out here in all this open space.

I'm starting to feel - what's the opposite of claustrophobic? I'm starting to feel that.

I'm also feeling the pace of living in rural Nevada. It's midday and between pulling up the weeds in the stall that morning and the two hour round trip for supplies and an impromptu smoothie run, I feel both exhausted and like

I haven't accomplished shit.

I smile at Gia, who takes everything in stride. I grab up my own smoothie- one of those healthy ones with kale and ginger that make Gia want to gag- and channel my inner enthusiast.

It's just a fence. You'll have it done by the end of the day and tomorrow you can rest.

Except I can't because tomorrow I have remote business meetings and paperwork to catch up on. Moving west doesn't mean I get to shirk my responsibilities back home. I channel some inner motivation by reminding myself that I can accomplish all that in my pajamas.

The light turns green and I inch us back up to highway speeds. I am focused once again on the road when Gia sits bolt upright and points out the window.

"Look!" She exclaims loudly, "dinosaurs!"

"What?" I'm taken off guard.

She's tapping on the passenger window. "Right there! That ranch has dinosaurs!"

And sure enough it does. As we pass by the entrance, I see metal pterodactyls perched on large cement pillars framing the entry gate. I can't get a good look as I split my attention between the ranch and light traffic, but I am pretty sure I see a T-Rex and a triceratops.

"Huh! Look at that!" I say, honestly impressed by their choice of landscape decoration. I also take note of the clean, organized rows of newly planted trees between the long neck and ourselves. Not a weed or sagebrush to be seen.

"Oh Em Gee! Dude! What if we have dinos on our ranch? And maybe people can even climb on them!" Gia is in full fixation mode now and if I don't pull her out, we'll end up with a space theme in there somewhere too.

"I think they've got the Jurassic period covered. But I'm sure you'll come up with a theme that is uniquely your own." I emphasize 'uniquely your own.' Stealing another ranch's aesthetic is not in good taste, however compelling it may be.

"I'll think on it," she says seriously, but her body is positively vibrating with the possibilities. She spends the rest of the drive on her phone, no doubt creating a new Pinterest inspiration board.

I gulp and focus on traffic, not on how much I am going to have my work cut out for me, chasing this one's imagination.

We pull up to the house with every intention of fixing the fence but as I look over at the rotting posts, all I see are more weeds. I could have sworn when we left we'd thoroughly picked every weed there was around that fence. It's as though the land is mocking me.

I look at Gia and she looks at me. "It's not so bad," she says, reading my mind. "We'll have it done by dinner."

"I like your gumption kid!" I say with an enthusiasm I don't feel.

We climb out of the truck and get to work removing wood planks and beams from its bed.

It's been years since working on my grandpa's ranch, but I remember helping him fix fences. I'd go section by section, pulling out one post, replacing it, then moving to the next. I see no reason why that method won't work for us here.

When the fresh wood is piled neatly on the hard-packed dirt, I get to work removing beams between the first two posts. They're so rotted they need no more than to be asked nicely before coming free. Gia has two down in the same amount of time I do. The posts are a bit more of a challenge and require both of us. I am surprised to learn each are anchored into the ground with cement. The fence is only five feet high yet the post is buried two feet down in solid cement.

"Alright, Gia, looks like we've hit our first dose of reality." I say, leaning a shoulder on the beam. I instantly regret it as I feel rough splinters grab hold of my shirt.

"Do we have to dig up all that cement?" She looks incredulous.

"Well, that depends." I shrug. I suspect she's about to learn a valuable life lesson.

"On what?" She goes to thrust the shovel into the ground, but the earth is too hard and rocky so the shovel slips and drops from her hand. She laughs and looks up at me in bemusement then just puts her hands on her hips like nothing happened.

"On whether or not you want to do the job right."

"So doing it wrong is an option?" She asks with a bit too much enthusiasm.

"Not if you want to keep a horse in here." I indicate the area inside the fence.

"So we dig," she concludes, already picking up the shovel.

"Yep." I sigh. "We dig."

* * *

Despite our best efforts, and the sweat and dirt covering us, by the time dinner rolls around, we have successfully removed a grand total of two posts. The shovel bouncing off the ground when Gia had tried to plant it should have been an omen. The earth here is unforgiving, resisting the sharp tip of the spade shovel or sending it sliding off rocks when we tried to dig deeper.

We both amble painfully into the house and plop down on the couch.

"I'm ordering pizza," I manage to say, though my arms will not raise my phone to complete the simple task.

"Double pepperoni," Gia mumbles then curls up into a ball.

"And root beer." I add wistfully. But the pizza and soda aren't ordering themselves so I force myself to sit up and dig my phone from my pocket.

"So," I say as I Google 'pizza near me,' "What do you think?"

"I can't think. I'm dead." Gia speaks into the pillow.

I reflect on the afternoon. Such a small amount of progress and yet every muscle in my body is screaming. I think about the cost versus the vision. It's such a big risk. And if we're really going to do this, we have to do it right.

"I know you wanted us to do this all ourselves…" I trail off, seeing how she responds to the insinuation.

"I changed my mind." Her exhausted voice comes through the pillow as, "eyeff shanged myff mine."

"I think once I've ordered the pizza it might be a good idea to give Chuck's friend a call. He might have a better plan of attack."

She says nothing but her arm raises and she gives me a thumbs up.

Good enough for me.

Ten

Keep It Cool

Beth

Cocoa and Hazel clomp down the trail on Carol's estate while we talk shop. It's only mid-morning but the April sun is already warm against our backs. Balancing on Cocoa with my thighs, I peel off my sweatshirt and tie it around my waist.

"I'm happy to stay on until August to transition clients over to you and ensure you've got your feet under you, but come end of summer, I intend to hit a tropical beach with a mai thai in hand and my cell phone back at the hotel room." Carol has a bounce to her voice that tells me she's more than ready to retire.

"Naturally! I think that's more than enough time." I navigate Cocoa around an overgrown brush. "We've already got a good start with the hand over, I doubt I'll even need that long but I'll take you for as long as you'll allow me to."

Carol laughs.

"Now, as we discussed, I'm leaving these two with you." She's referring to our current riding companions. "You tell me if it's too much, and be honest. How do you feel about keeping Pepper and Biscuit until I get back? They'll join me in Bishop when I return, but I'd hate to leave them in unfamiliar hands while I'm gone."

I smile. Here I am, worried about how well her clients will take to me, what with me having a different therapy style and lacking that tough motherly love that seems to work for her clients. She's thinking horses, horses, horses. She either has a ton of faith in my abilities as a therapist, or she really loves her animals. Probably both.

I laugh. "I'll keep them as long as you need me to!"

"I appreciate it."

Before we can continue, a large dark blob shoots out of the bush in front of us. Cocoa rears up and begins to panic as the mastiff mix wags its tail and barks relentlessly, bouncing from side to side on the trail in front of us.

Cocoa snorts and stomps, which seems to encourage the dog closer. It runs around the side of us, out of Cocoa's sight, sending Cocoa into a panic. He jolts forward and turns, looking for the interloper. I nearly fall off, but manage to keep my balance and center myself back into the saddle.

I lean into Cocoa practically laying against his neck and rubbing, reassuring him while slowly backing him up and bringing him back around. He's skittish, but seems to listen to my soothing.

"There, there, its just a doggie," I say quietly. "He just wants to say 'hi' and doesn't have good manners."

The mastiff has decided the horses are too big for playmates, but is still circling close by and barking, it's butt up in the air and tail wagging. Not vicious, but still dangerous around horses.

Out of the corner of my eye, I see Carol handling Hazel. Seems the dog set off both beasts, but they remain relatively calm, skipping out of the way, but not rearing up or bolting. Gypsy would have been somewhere up in the mountains by now, my ass dumped in a sagebrush somewhere along the way.

"Apollo!" I hear a voice call over the relentless barking. "Get over here, Apollo!"

A young woman approaches from down the trail, but the horses are between her and her dog. She's smart enough not to try to pass through us.

"Over there," I say to Carol and point to a side trail. It's a smaller foot trail, but it'll do to get us out of the way.

"Come, Apollo, come!" She's shouting, clearly stressed out. "Sorry!" She calls to us. "He's just a puppy. He's usually good off leash, but he's never seen horses before."

"I'm sure he is," Carol says as she keeps careful control of the reins. "But this is a horse trail so he really oughtta be on leash."

Carol and I navigate enough out of the way that the woman can reach Apollo and get him properly leashed.

"Yeah, I'm so sorry," She says again. Her face is bright red and she looks down at the sand. "We come out here every day and I've never see anyone on horseback."

"No harm done," I say. "He just needs a little work. If you like taking him out here, just get him accustomed to horses and he'll be fine."

Carol leans over to me and whispers, "Good thing my animals are dog trained."

I laugh, but in truth, my heart is still racing from the encounter. Adrenaline, sure, but it's something more than that. I've been unsteady lately—not just on horseback.

I think about that stranger in the coffee shop. William "Bill" Fitzgerald. Still not sure how I let myself feel anything for him—whether I liked his charm or was just caught off guard by it. Probably doesn't matter. He's not part of the plan.

But damn if the thought doesn't keep circling back, stubborn as a loose rein.

Once Apollo and his mortified owner are off down the trail behind us, we take back to the trail, continuing in the opposite direction. I'm still catching my breath but Carol seems unaffected.

"You're good with people *and* with animals, which makes you a rare breed."

I don't know what to say. My confidence had been so shaken before coming here that it's nice to have it bolstered. "Aww...thanks Carol!"

"I'm serious, girl. I was beginning to think I'd never be able to retire, but then you came around. I can't think of a better person to take over for me." She looks at me under the brim of her hat and I feel something like a motherly pride emanating from her.

That makes me feel good. I'm not just swooping in and nabbing up her business. I'm carrying on her legacy.

* * *

I get a call just as I pull out of Carol's ranch.

"Hey, Mom," I answer in a sing-song tone.

"Hey, Sweetie! You sound happy!"

You sound happy that I'm happy I observe.

"Yeah! Just finished up with Carol and Chuck, and you know what, I think I've really got this." I hadn't realized how many doubts I had until I was sitting there at Carol's kitchen table talking numbers over coffee and it suddenly became more real.

"Oh, I know you do!" My cheerleader mother exclaims.

"Thanks, Mom. But hey, you called me. So what's up?" I pull out onto East Valley, a long road that runs through most of the length of the valley, parallel to the highway.

"Oh, not much. I'm out of bird feed. Do you think you could stop at the feed store and pick some up for me on your way home?"

My mom, the humanitarian. Or is it birditarian? No, that sounds too much like someone who only eats birds. That woman can't stop *feeding* them. I tease her that should she suddenly die, so would half the valley's bird population.

"Sure, Mom, no problem!" I check the time. It's early enough that I can pick it up and still get a nap in before hitting a few office tasks.

"Thanks, honey, you're the best! Oh! And tonight we'll celebrate you being one step closer to owning your very own horse ranch!" She sounds just as giddy as I feel.

"Mom, there's still a little way to go. Let's save the celebration for when I sign the contract." I'm optimistic, to be sure, but this is my big restart. I don't want to curse the damn thing!

"Okay, fine," she says with fake despondency. "I'm still going to cook you up a roasted chicken and you can't say no to chocolate chip cookies."

"No," I tease because I know it will drive her crazy.

"They're not to celebrate. I'm just using up some leftover chocolate chips. I was going to make them anyway."

I chuckle at the woman's tenacity.

"Sounds good. I'll see you soon."

So off to the feed store. Not for livestock feed, mind you. For bird feed. I alter my course slightly, cutting into town instead of skirting along it.

Eleven

Meet Not-Cute

Will

I don't know what I'm doing.

I'm standing in a random aisle of the feed store, staring at an overwhelming wall of miscellaneous garden tools and supplies that might as well be ancient runes. I've got a busted hinge in my pocket—rusted, bent, and held together by pure spite—and somehow that's still not helping me figure out what size I need.

I passed something that might've been post hole diggers a few aisles back, or maybe they were weapons. Hard to say.

I rub the back of my neck and try not to sigh out loud. I should've looked this up ahead of time. Should've brought Gia. Hell, I should've hired someone. But I've been buried in construction quotes, permit checklists, and sleepless nights trying to convince myself this whole thing isn't a mistake.

I'm still muttering about galvanized steel versus powder-coating when I catch a flicker of movement across the aisle.

And just like that, there she is.

Beth. Coffee shop flirt and concert critic with her sharp wit and soft cheekbones. She's carrying two massive bags of birdseed like they weigh nothing. Her hair's pulled back, loose strands escaping like she couldn't be bothered to worry about it, and her jeans are caked with a hint of dried mud. There's a precision to the way she moves that reminds me of someone who gets shit done.

I clear my throat. "Beth?"

She turns. Her eyebrows lift. "Hey. Will, right?"

Right. A fact she didn't seem to fond to discover.

"Yeah, that's right." I nod, trying not to look like I just walked into a surprise party. "Didn't expect to see you here."

"The feed store's kind of the town's social hub," she replies, dry as the Nevada wind. She nods toward my empty cart. "You looking for irrigation?"

It takes me a second. I glance behind me.

Garden hoses.

"Oh—uh, no. Fence repair. Or something like that." I fish the warped hinge from my pocket. "Trying to replace these. One of the gates broke."

She eyes the hinge like it insulted her horse. "That's not salvageable."

"No?" I ask, like I hadn't just spent the last fifteen minutes debating it.

She adjusts the birdseed bags. "Fence hardware's back aisle, end cap near the fencing wire. Look for livestock-rated sets."

I blink. "Would you mind showing me?"

She hesitates—barely a beat—but then turns and starts walking. Not exactly warm, but not hostile either. I follow.

She moves like she knows this place inside and out. No wasted motion. No unnecessary chatter. I like that. I like the way she scans the shelves, selects a few hinge options, and explains the difference in coating and load bearing without slowing down.

"You'll want something with at least a 400-pound load capacity," she says, handing me a reinforced pair of hinges. "And maybe actual tools this time."

Ouch. That one's fair.

"I should probably get a post hole digger too," I mutter.

"Aisle ten. Second row."

"And a flashlight?"

She gives me a look. Then she points—to the shelf directly beside us.

I grin, caught. "Yeah. I walked past that one."

"Mmhmm." She nods, but I catch a trace of a smile at the corner of her mouth.

There's a pause. Not quite awkward. Not warm either. I'm not sure if she's holding back or just doesn't give a damn. Either way, I kind of respect it.

"You've saved me from wandering in circles," I say. "Thanks."

She shifts the seed bags in her arms. "If you get lost again, talk to Tom. He's in grooming. Been here since the Reagan administration."

Message received.

"Right. Will do."

I watch as she turns toward checkout, calm and efficient, not even waiting for a goodbye.

Interesting woman.

The type to keep her guard up. To work hard. To handle her own fence repair, probably better than I could. She's not warm and bubbly. She doesn't flirt or fawn. But she's smart. And solid. And something about that just hit different.

I look down at the hinge in my hand.

Game on.

Twelve

Certified? Or Certifiable

Beth

I click "End Session" and lean back in my chair with a sigh. The soft chime of Zoom closing is the only sound in the room for a moment. My laptop screen returns to the desktop where a woman at the top of a mountain stands triumphant. I'd done the hike last summer with my Bay Area besties, Lucas and Shar, back when I felt like I was on top of the world. I see her in contrast to the ghostly reflection of my present self—a vaguely tired version: professional blouse still crisp, makeup clinging on, headset askew.

I pull the headset off and rub my temples. "Alright, Lexis," I mutter to the empty room, "you had a big breakthrough. Now it's my turn."

Lexis had come through something big, and today's session was mostly celebration. I'm proud of him—and of myself. I'm feeling drained, but in that satisfying, getting-the-work-done kind of way. And somewhere under the fatigue, a realization is taking root: this can really work.

In a single motion, I shrug out of the tan knit cardigan that was passing as professional attire. It slides off and lands over the back of the chair, revealing a ribbed tank top and the comfy, dust-covered jeans I've had on since sunrise.

Superman shedding Clark Kent.

Certified? Or Certifiable

One part virtual therapist, one part horse whisperer. Silicon Valley meets Wild Wild West.

The thought of it makes me think of giant mechanical spiders and now I want one. I laugh out loud as I reach for a blue binder with the word **EAGALA** printed across the front in bold brown letters. Equine-assisted therapy doesn't come without a mountain of coursework and checklists, but I'm checking the boxes. Slowly.

I head out into the sunlight, where Gypsy waits at the fence, ears swiveling like she's been expecting me. I grab a halter in one hand and a fistful of treats in the other.

"Okay, girl. You ready to work?"

She snorts.

"I hear ya." I rub her nose and clip the halter. "Remember, we're both in training. So go easy on me, okay?"

Technically, the certification is for me—I'm the one proving my ability to lead therapeutic sessions with an equine counterpart—but she's got a checklist of her own: safety, temperament, responsiveness. We start with basic exercises, including standing pretty, raising hooves, longeing. She nails them. Then I guide her through stretches, watching for posture, body tension. She's relaxed and focused.

"Alright, Gyps. Today's patient is me. Let's get to it."

A motorcycle engine revs down the street, sending her into a nervous dance. I steady her, murmuring reassurances, and when she calms, I pat her side.

"Looks like we've gotta work on distractions. Both of us."

"A year ago, I had a clear path." I tack her up as I talk, more for my own benefit than hers. "Steady clients, a practice in the City by the Bay, a partner to build my dreams with. I thought I was building something solid. Turns out it was built on sand."

I tighten a strap and sigh.

Gypsy doesn't answer, which is part of her charm. She lets me fidget, lets me rant, lets me suck at things without judgment. And right now, I suck at tacking. My fingers are clumsy and my shoulders already ache.

I grunt as I lift the saddle. "Oof. Still out of shape."

Once everything's in place, I rest my hands on her back.

"If I were the therapist here, what would I say?"

I pause, then answer myself aloud.

"You're not starting over. You're starting different. With experience. With purpose."

That feels true. I say it again, softer. Then I mount, slow and steady, and take a breath.

She's so easy to guide around the fenced-in area, I barely need the reins. I feel her strength beneath me and channel it. Straighten my back. Reclaim the girl I used to be, but better this time. Wiser. Weathered. Always learning.

A face flashes across my mind. Brown eyes. Heart-stopping smile. A pristine cowboy hat and an aura too clean for how dusty he actually was. There was something about him—something that made my stomach flutter. Until it didn't.

Recalling the concert, I clench my jaw. But I am proud of my cool, calm performance in the feed store when what I really wanted to do was deck the guy.

"Well, Gyps," I mutter, "at least I saw through this guy's charade early on."

I shift my weight to the right. She adjusts like a dream.

"Hey! Not bad!"

I grin, but the thought still lingers: why do I keep falling for the wrong ones? Chuck seems like a great guy. He's decent, grounded, and ego-free. Why don't I get all mushy over someone like that? Awkward but dependable.

"Maybe I need to think with my head and not my hormones."

Gypsy flicks an ear back toward me in annoyance. I chuckle.

"Don't worry, girl. You've got a special spot in the center of my heart."

We head out the back gate and onto the trail. The sun's still high, the sky that perfect Nevada blue, and I can feel my own energy starting to shift.

"This is the life I'm building. Me and you." I remember the dog on the trail the other day. "And maybe another fur buddy to nip at your heels and get me jogging."

Gypsy steps lightly along the hard-packed sand, and I know she's listening in the way horses do.

"You know what?" I tell her as contentment settles into my soul, "You're going to make an excellent therapy horse."

Thirteen

Reinforcements Arrive

Will

A clean cut man with glasses, pleated tan shorts, and a white polo shirt is the last thing I expect to see climbing out of the ten-year-old pick up. Ben Wilkes, ranch hand extraordinaire, looks more like a retired broker heading to a golf tournament. Not what I expected. I thought this guy worked with his hands.

I hope Chuck is right about him.

I lean a rake up against the half-repaired horse fence and pull off my leather work gloves.

"Ben Wilkes," I say, squinting into the afternoon sun. Then it hits me— From the concert. Beth's dad. Shit.

"So I hear." He jokes back.

He looks different without the pressed flannel, cowboy hat, and a beer in his hand. I'm pretty sure he had a good helping of stubble then too, didn't he? The details come to mind in stark clarity. There was beer, groups of people laughing, and Beth insulting me behind my back- that one stung more than I'd care to admit.

After the look she gave me at the concert, I'm not sure how I feel about working with her father. What are the odds she hasn't built me up to be the world's greatest fool? I didn't even say goodbye. Hell, I barely said hello. Not exactly the kind of impression you want to leave with a girl's family, even if she *did* act like I was dog crap stuck to her boot.

I point and put on my best business charm smile while trying not to grimace. "You were at the concert the other night."

"I remember you as well. Chuck's friend who doesn't like dancing." He takes my hand and gives it a solid shake. Now *that* feels like the hands of a guy who's built something. Rough calluses and a muscular grip. Things I am suddenly acutely aware I may lack.

I laugh—awkward, forced. "Yeah, I was… distracted." I wave it off like it doesn't matter. "Spent most of the night worrying about my sister."

Ben nods slowly, probably clocking the tension coming off me like steam. He coughs into his hand and says, "So, what can I do ya for?"

I exhale, grateful for the change of subject. I don't know how much this guy knows about me—or what his daughter's told him—but I can't afford to make a fool of myself. Not today. Not with this much on the line.

"Are you the ranch guy?" A perky voice shouts across the yard before I can answer.

Gia barrels around the corner on her bike like a bat outta hell, dust trailing behind her. She skids to a stop inches from Ben, wild-eyed and grinning, her elbow scraped raw and her shirt half-torn from sagebrush.

My stomach clenches and my jaw drops. "Gia, what happened?"

"Nothing," she shrugs, dismounting with all the swagger of a cowboy and knocking the kickstand down with the toe of her foot.

I cross my arms and narrow my eyes at the chunks of sagebrush bark stuck to the shoulder of her shirt and what I am almost positive is a bloody elbow.

"What? I fell. It wasn't a big deal. I was coming down a hill and my tire hit a rock and I spilled. I'm fine." She dusted her shirt off, somehow missing all the clinging plant matter.

Ben chuckled. "Looks like you had yourself some fun." He turned to me. "Kids. They like to learn the hard way. This one yours?"

I hesitate.

"Yes and no. Ben, this is my little sister, Gianna. Gia, this is Ben, the 'Ranch Guy.'"

If I even had a modicum of control over the situation since Ben arrived, I lose it now, to the fire and spunk of a teenager with a dream.

"Yay! Great! I have so many ideas and so many questions!"

At least she has the wherewithal to hold out a hand, although I doubt he'll want to shake one that dirty.

He takes her hand with the same firmness he'd taken mine and gives it a sturdy shake. Gia's body loses balance for a moment, but I watch her square up and return the shake heartily.

I crack a smile.

"Well, Gianna-" Ben starts.

"Oh, you can call me Gia. Sometimes Will calls me Gigi but I only like it when he calls me that." Then her voice drops. "Or when my parents used to."

A painful chord strikes in my heart. I take half a step toward her, but Ben is already on it.

"I am sorry to hear about your loss. There's none greater than losing a parent or a child. I can promise you one thing. You'll never stop thinking about them or missing them, but it does get easier." He narrows his eyes, weighing the change in Gia's posture. "You know what, Gia?"

She looks up at him, shoulders still haunched. "What?"

"There is no better tribute to your parents than building something big, beautiful, and your own. And you've got a sharp eye. This property is perfect for the task."

She looks up beaming. "You think so too, huh?"

I look around, confused. *This property? Perfect? He must be trying to make her feel better.*

"Well, yeah, just look at its position. East side of the valley, but not too close to the eastern ridge, slightly elevated. You've got one of the best views of the valley. And I'll bet the sunrises and sunsets are magnificent from here."

"That's what I was thinking!" Gia's smile beams ear to ear as she fidgets excitedly.

"Come on, why don't you show me around." Ben holds his hands out,

Reinforcements Arrive

waiting for Gia to lead the way.

I follow as well, but I have officially become part of the background. It is the Gia and Ben show now and I am just a side character. The financier. I gulp, but hold on to a shred of hope. Maybe once Ben sees the state of the property and not just its position compared with the sun, he will give her a good dose of reality about the amount of work cut out for her.

Gia skips the house all together and goes straight for the horse corral. I cringe. Our handiwork is right there on display. Torn up fence posts, half unburied cement anchors, piles of new wood, already catching tumbleweeds and leaves in the afternoon winds, and the two posts we managed to install since I'd reached out to him.

Ben looks sideways at me and raises an eyebrow. I put my fist up to my mouth to hide my guilty smile and I shrug. But when he asks about the fence, he asks Gia.

I feel my stomach tighten. It's her project, but I am used to being the one in charge, used to answering the questions and giving direction. She's just a teen. Her answers should be vetted through me first.

"I really want to get a horse," she explained, "so we figured we'd start here."

"So you're tearing the whole thing up, huh?" He put one hand on his hip and the other on his chin.

"It's rotting." I explain, glad to be able to show that I know what I am doing.

"You don't say," Ben mused.

I can't begin to interpret his meaning

Approaching the fence, he examines each of our new posts, rubbing a thumb over the nails. Then he pulls a folding knife *out of the pocket of his tan polo shorts.*

"Screws, not nails," Ben says as he uses the edge of his knife to pop the nail right out. "And these are too short, even for nails." Of course it's screws. I nod like I knew that all along.

"Yeah, I just used what the guy before me did." It's a lame scapegoat but the best I could come up with on the fly.

"See, now, that would be your first mistake. Don't always trust the work of the man before you. You gotta check. Taking out the posts, just the two of you? That'd be your second. Not setting the new posts in cement-"

"My third?" I wager a guess. I am used to doing business with men twice as intelligent as I am and I concede that this is squarely Ben's area of expertise, not mine, but I still feel a significant blow to my ego.

He clicks his tongue and winks.

I can see where Beth gets her sharp wit and sharper intellect.

Gia is clearly now better educated but unimpressed. I watch as she shifts her weight from side to side, looking at the stalls and the open fields beyond. She wants to show off her dream, not talk about fence hardware.

"Some of these posts were replaced recently, including that one over there," he motions to one of the two we'd already pulled. "They'll just need some sanding and sealing against the weather."

"So that means less work, right?" She puts in hopefully.

Ben laughs. "I don't know about less work. Different work." He stands up straight and turns back to face us. "So horses here. Easy 'nuff. What's next?"

Gia releases all the pent up energy at once, springing into action. "Over here! I want to put in a petting area thing and a chicken coop."

Ben excuses himself, saunters back to his truck, and returns with a note pad. This just went from fixing a fence or two to landscaping and building. I assume he is beginning to see the scope of it. I wait for him to give his opinion on the ideas, maybe knock a few down, but he simply acknowledges her ideas and gestures for her to move on.

Gia lights up. Ben's taking notes. I'm just trying not to look like I'm just the idiot with a bank account.

At the back of the property Gia leads us to a place where the ground dips, creating a dry, dusty bowl.

"And here I am thinking a duck pond."

That's a new one.

"Woa, Gia-" I start to say, but Ben is already talking.

"Great place for one. You could build a gazebo on the north end where it flattens out."

"Yes!" Gia holds her hands out, sweeping them across the landscape as

Reinforcements Arrive

she explains, "I see a trail, leading from the house and around the pond so people can go on morning walks."

"You got a good eye and a sharp mind, kid," Ben says as he scribbles more notes.

Great.

By the time we make it back to the house the sun is resting a couple of inches above the mountain peak and a chilly wind has picked up. Gia's vision of Gardnerville's one and only guest ranch has been meticulously, enthusiastically communicated to Ben and he's got himself a good three pages of notes.

Watching Ben's cool demeanor as Gia explains every little thing she wants to do, gives my nervous system permission to relax, just a little. Yet when we settle down around the kitchen table, my nagging doubts are still in charge.

"So," I say, folding my arms on the table in front of me, "pretty bad, isn't it?"

"I'd say not bad at all. Sure, you've got more than your fair share of sagebrush to tear through and some trash removal, but the land itself is what really counts and underneath the clutter you've got a strong backbone."

"Really…" My thoughts begin to shift as his words sink in.

"Oh sure! Your buildings are sturdy and sound, your fences need some fixing but that is par for the course on any property out here. Some landscaping to give it a face lift, a little sweat, blood, and tears for structures like the gazebo. With a little hard work, you could have it up and running by the end of summer."

"Did you say blood?" Gia leaned in, her brow furrowed.

"Oh it's just an expression. Hard work is all. And you can always contract it out. In fact—" He turns the pages to the front of his notebook and begins reviewing the timeline for the overall project and breaking down each task.

Just then, Gia pipes up, "What about the duck pond?"

Ben pauses mid-note.

I stiffen. *Ah, crap.*

"Well," Ben says slowly, "you'd need to pipe in water, and that means permits—state, most likely. Depending on the size, you're looking at significant excavation, water rights, inspections... Might be a phase two kind of project."

Gia's smile drops. "But that's where the ducks go."

Ben gives her a gentle shrug. "Doesn't mean never. Just not yet. That part of the land's still beautiful without water."

"But it's called Duck Pond," Gia insists.

"Then let's call it Duck Hollow," Ben replies gently. He leans toward her in a fatherly gesture. "Dreams are often built in layers. Start with the foundation now, and let the water come later."

Gia bites her lip, clearly trying not to sulk. Then she nods. "Okay. Duck Hollow. But I want a sign."

Ben grins. "I know a guy."

I gotta say, this man makes ranch work look easy.

* * *

Less than an hour later, we wave Ben off, and Gia bolts inside—already plotting her evening raid with her online crew.

I stay outside, letting the late-afternoon chill settle over me as the sun dips behind the mountains. The light spills gold over the valley. Soft. Peaceful. Damn near beautiful.

Golden Hour, Gia called it. She was right.

I glance around the property again, this time seeing the outlines of what could be. I ignore what is—piles of junk, broken fences, half-buried dreams—and focus on what could be. A ranch. A haven. A fresh start.

We could have stayed in Newport Beach. Or moved to Texas. Gone back to Grandpa's polished legacy under Aunt Cathy's manicured thumb. It is the safe choice, predictable. But Gia wants her own legacy, complete with her version of wild. Her own name on the gate. After a lifetime of working in

Reinforcements Arrive

the family business, I can't say that I blame her. Hell, I might even admire her.

Aunt Cathy said it was a fool's errand. Maybe it is, but standing here, dust on my jeans, calluses forming, I feel more grounded than I have in years.

And for the first time, I realize I don't want to do it alone.

My mind flickers to Beth. That sharp tongue. Those steel eyes. The way her voice curls around a sentence like a lasso.

"Not happening," I mutter. Though stranger things have happened.

I tuck my gloves into my back pocket and head inside. The ranch won't build itself.

Fourteen

Chop Wood, Carry Water

Beth

Hot chamomile and honey run down my throat, warming me from the inside. I lean back on my parent's padded patio chair and put my head up to the sky. It's alight with brilliant orange, dark purples creeping in on the shadowed sides of the clouds.

I pull my fleece-lined jacket tighter around me against the afternoon spring breeze then take a long sip of my tea. The desert is so dependent upon the sun that the temperature drops into cold the moment its yellow orb touches Jobs Peak. Which it just officially has.

After a long day of horse training and people therapisting, it feels good to just relax and take in a quiet moment. The contrast between city and country living is not lost on me. Early evenings in the city can be a different kind of peaceful, but they're never quiet. The hum of traffic and sporadic sounds of life forever surround you. I draw in deep breaths between sips of fragrant tea, feeling the serene peace of rural living sink into me.

That is, until my mind is unoccupied enough to let all the thoughts in. Tonight they're heavy, all about past failures and the uncertainty of the future. It could be that today's review of Peaceful Spirit's financials left me with feelings of uncertainty. Or it could just be the weight of all the changes I made in such a short period, sitting like boulders on my chest. Either way, I am grateful for the break in my spiraling reverie when I hear Dad's truck pull across the gravel on the side of their - our? - house.

I shake off my fears with an exercise I often give my clients, one that gets them grounded in the moment. I focus on my senses and take inventory. Even far from the city, the world around me is rich with sensation. I pick up on the smells of my tea, the shampoo in my hair as it blows across my face, and dust and sagebrush, tinged with the earthy, grassy smell of the horses.

I've moved through things I can see, which could keep me busy the rest of the night, and am on hearing, when I hear the glass door slide open. A new, yet familiar smell hits me: tacos. Mom and I made them for dinner and left a plate for Dad in the microwave.

"Hey, Dad," I say without looking back.

"Hey yourself, Pumpkin." He responds as he comes around the wicker chair and settles into the cushion beside me. "What has you hiding out here tonight?"

He picks up a dripping tortilla stuffed with shredded chicken and takes a bite.

I mimic his action by taking a sip then look out over the back of the property up to the mountains beyond.

"Not hiding. Just taking a minute to myself."

"Bullshit," he retorts, playful yet stern, "When you were younger, you used to come out here and sit when you had something to think through."

I hate how well this man knows me. But I also love it.

"I don't know, Dad, everything just feels so…big right now. I feel like I've lost a part of myself and now I am someone completely different. It's destabilizing."

"You know, losing yourself happens from time to time." His statement is the poster child of matter-of-fact. He scoops a spoonful of black beans up into his mouth then adds, "We all gotta go through it."

"You and Mom never went through anything like this." I retort, refusing to hear what he is trying to tell me. "I mean, I am back in the town I grew up in. Living with *my parents*."

"Oh, you don't know the half of it." he chuckles as he fiddles wayward lettuce and chicken back into their soft shell. "You remember that Christmas when you were ten?"

"The one with the swing set?" I furrow my brow and pull my knees in under me against the encroaching chill.

"That's the one. Did you know, your uncle Chris paid for all of it." He looks at me sideways, one eyebrow raised and lips tucked in tight.

"What? No! I didn't know that. Why?"

"That was the year the ranch went under and I lost my job. We spent through our savings just paying bills and looking after you girls. We didn't want you to feel the impact so we kept up the spending and by the time Christmas rolled around, we were flat broke." He took another big bite of soggy taco. "We almost lost the house, but he helped us with that, too." He's completely at ease, as though talking about the weather, while discussing the almost ruin of our family twenty two years ago.

"I thought you had work lined up already!" My retort is lame, but I am still processing. That, and the mention of Silver Sage Ranch brings to mind a certain billionaire who takes sport in playing with people's feelings.

"I did too, but it fell through. Then winter hit and no one was hiring. I was out of a job for eight months."

"How did I not know about this?" I squeak.

"We didn't want you girls to worry." Dad shrugs. "But listen, the point isn't that we went through a hard time. The point is, it was hard. I felt like a failure, like I'd let down myself and my family. But I got through it."

And so will you. I add the last, unspoken bit.

I wrap my hands around the hot mug and let out a long sigh.

"It just- everything feels like too much. I mean, how did I not see it coming?"

The way he sighs sounds empathetic. He places his hand on my knee and says sternly, "First, he made damn sure you didn't see it coming so you'd do well to stop blaming yourself for someone else's behavior."

"Yeah." I frown.

"Second, you have loving family, just like your mom and I did, who can hold you up and carry you through the hard times." He patted my knee as he spoke then went back to his plate.

The therapist in me nodded along. The hurt woman in me crossed her arms and pouted.

"I should be able to take care of myself."

Now he just laughs.

"I know, I know." And I do know, but I look at the sky as it darkens into a deep red and trudge forward with my stubborn mope. "But I didn't just almost lose everything. I *lost* everything, including my dignity and self-respect."

"Yet here you are. Alive, healthy, safe, surrounded by people who love you and with an amazing opportunity in front of you."

"So how do I get from here to there?" I sigh and take a long swig of my quickly cooling chamomile.

"That part's easy. Chop wood, carry water." He picks his plate back up and gets to work on the Spanish rice.

"Huh?"

"Sometimes, when life gets too heavy, you gotta zero in on what's really important. Identify the next step then do it. Fuck the past. It's in the past. You just keep chopping your wood. Every. Single. Day."

"So I ignore my problems?" I am incredulous.

"No, you accept your problems. And don't let them swallow you whole."

I remain silent for a long time, letting it all soak in. I realize I was just about to dive into the rabbit hole, but my dad yanked me right back out. But the peek down memory lane was not in vain. Because he's right. Chop wood, carry water. The advice is not about my past, it's about my future and how to get there. Finally I take in a long breath and slap my knee.

"So, Ben Willkes, how was your day?"

He looks at me seriously, no doubt ensuring that the momentary crisis has passed, then laughs.

"Oh, it was fine. Took Dancer and Grumpy out with Jane this morning." Dancer was Jane's horse. Grumpy, my dad's, is aptly named because my dad is the only person on God's green earth that he tolerates.

He continues, "Then I stopped in at the Fitzgerald Ranch to offer the kid a little help."

Calling Will a kid makes me feel oddly vindicated. Like I'm not the only one who sees him as childish.

"Ugh," I groan. "How bad is it out there?"

"Funny, Will asked me the same question." He scoops up the last of the rice and beans then sits his plate on the glass patio table next to him.

I roll my eyes. "To think I almost liked the guy."

"Eh, well, you're in recovery. None of your emotions are settled. Maybe taking a step back from liking guys isn't a bad idea. Focus on carrying those buckets. There's time enough for that later."

I scoff.

"Not if you ask Mom. She thinks I need to be married with a handful of crotch goblins, like, yesterday."

I'm grateful for my dad. I feel like he gets me.

"Oh, she just thinks the answer to falling off the horse is to get back on. It broke her heart to see you crushed. You ask me, I think she believes that you not getting back into dating means you're not moving on."

"And you agree with her?" I ask tentatively, my lips stopped on the edge of my wide-brimmed tea cup.

"Absolutely not." He shakes his head. "Your mother thinks the answer is to find the next guy. I think the answer is to find yourself first. The rest will come naturally."

"My dad the philosopher." I snuggle up against him, laying my head on his shoulder.

My heart swells for the man, up into my throat, forcing out a tear from my eye. Hearts can do that, you know.

"You're doing just fine, Beth. Life didn't throw you lemons, it dropped a damn lemon tree right down on top of you. And look at you now, about to start your very own practice."

"Is that the lemonade?" I giggle, sniffing and wiping away the tear.

"Nope, that's just the squeeze. The lemonade is becoming the woman you decide you want to be." He wraps his arm around me, bringing my head off his shoulder and onto his cologned chest. *Old Spice.* I breath it in and wrap my arms around him too.

Every woman deserves a dad like Ben Wilkes.

***

When we come inside, tea and tacos consumed and chill having hit our bones, my mom is snuggled up on the couch, crocheting while watching one of her crime-solving dramas. Looking at her I realize I have a new appreciation for her.

I walk behind the couch and put my arms around her neck.

"I love you, Mom," I say into her hair.

"I love you, too, sweet thing." She turns her head up and kisses my cheek.

I kiss her head and pull away. "Have a good night." I look up at the screen. It looks like CSI or Law and Order- hell, I don't know. But I add anyway, "The sister did it."

I keep walking down the hall as she says, "Beth! No spoilers!"

"Night, Mom!"

"Night!"

And with that, the world is right and Beth Wilkes is off to sleep. Tomorrow, I take my first step toward finding myself again. Chop wood, carry water. That'll be enough.

Fifteen

Wine Walk

Beth

It's May. In Gardnerville, that means the third Thursday of the month just got better—this one specifically. It's the first Wine Walk of the season, and you bet your ass I'm there. Local restaurants and businesses line the streets, their tables offering crafts, swag, and, for the alcohol-consumers, a taste from their wine selection. People come out in droves—walking, laughing, sampling.

Jane and I are two of them, weaving through booths and tasting stations until we spot the Overland table. I recognize the woman bent over rummaging in a plastic storage bin. Black curls, bold stance—definitely Cassie. Jane told me on the way over that she used to teach Cassie private dance lessons back when Cassie was a teenager. She even competed for a while, and they still keep in touch loosely. Tonight, she's bartending and got roped into manning the table.

"Cassie!" I shout enthusiastically.

She straightens, holding two vases full of plastic flowers, and sets them on the table like they've personally offended her.

"Beth? Is that you?" She squints into the sun.

"In the flesh," I say, turning my hip to model a new spring dress and knee-high boots.

"Holy shit! Jane told me you were back in town! How the hell are ya?" Her smile is wide and sincere. "And hi Jane! Come here you lovely bitch!"

Jane practically skips into her arms.

When I left, I lost touch with nearly everyone. Small-town slow and big-city fast don't always keep pace. Jane and Cassie stayed loosely connected through messages and seasonal catch-ups, and now here I am—benefiting from Jane's steadiness.

Cassie wraps me in a warm, teddy-bear hug like no time has passed. Then she's back to pulling items from her bin.

"Ugh, stuck at the table all night. Jackston called in and guess who gets to rack in some overtime?" She spreads her arms wide and flashes a dramatic fake smile.

"Wait," Jane puts a hand to her temple. "Let me guess. Jerry?"

"Fuck off!" Cassie punches Jane's arm. "You got your Forever Glasses?"

"I sure do." I hold up the glass that will carry me through another wine walk season.

"Yep," Jane echoes, brandishing her own.

"You need help setting up?" I offer. I know frazzled when I see it.

"Nah, I got it. I owe that fucker one anyway." She rolls her eyes and turns back to Jane. "Did you hear what happened at the last Town Hall meeting?"

"Nooooo, what?" Jane answers in her best *tell me everything* voice.

Politics isn't my area of gossip, but whatever gets them going.

"I'm going in for drinks," I announce—but they're already deep in the drama.

By the time I return with drinks, they've shifted topics.

"Oh my god, did you see the guy from the Appeal article?" Cassie fans herself with a handful of fliers. "That smile. Those forearms. *Oof.*"

Just behind us, I catch part of a conversation drifting from the next booth.

"They say he paid cash," a woman murmurs.

"For the whole ranch?"

"Yep. Showed up outta nowhere and threw down like he's buying a vacation home."

I peek over. Trish Donnelly—my old Home Ec teacher—is talking to someone I don't know, probably from the library board where she chairs. "Can't buy history," Trish says with a sniff. "No matter how nice the jeans fit."

Jane snorts, dragging my attention back.

"You're so shallow."

"Says the woman who practically swoons when Chuck talks tax assessments," Cassie fires back, arching one perfectly sculpted brow—the kind of brow that says she has Opinions and the tweezers to back them up.

"Okay, valid."

Cassie glances at me. "Beth, didn't you say you knew him?"

"What?" I blink. "Who?"

"That guy who bought the Fitzgerald place. Will something-or-other."

Will. The guy I can't seem to escape. I'm still reeling from the overheard chatter.

"So I keep hearing. And yeah, we've met." I try to keep the frown off my face. It was just a few quick interactions. Nothing significant.

Cassie smirks. "Girl, your face just did a whole thing."

Jane perks up, catching on. "Ohhh no. Wait—wait. *Do you like him?*"

"I do *not* like him," I say, already regretting everything.

Cassie grins. "Too late. You totally *do*. Oh my god. You'd be so hot together."

Jane groans. "She's shipping it."

"Fully. I ship it *hard*," Cassie nods decisively. "Sunshine and brooding cowboy energy? I'd read that book."

I down half my glass of wine.

"Speak of the devil," Jane says, eyes wide. She nods toward the sidewalk.

My body zaps with nerves before I even turn.

I finally look. Crisp shirt, sleeves rolled, tailored jeans like sin. He's smiling, interacting, admiring art, petting a basset hound, adjusting a crooked sign.

Of course he's charming *and* helpful.

I look at Jane, who's laughing and pretending to be immersed in Cassie's commentary. Through clenched teeth, I say, "Kill me."

"Oh come on, he's not that bad," Cassie says, arms crossed, giving him a once-over like he's the dessert menu at Overland.

"Oh! Chuck is with him!" Jane claps her hands like it's a double feature.

"Well…" I say.

"Well what?" Jane narrows her eyes.

"Aren't you gonna go get him?" Cassie nudges Jane, who gives her a gentle shove.

Too late. They're already heading this way.

A replay of the concert flashes through my mind with every step Will takes. At least this time, I see him coming.

Behave yourself Beth. Act cool.

I put on a smile and ensure that I am the first one to greet them.

"Hi, Chuck!" I say first, then deliberately turn my gaze to Will. "Will. Nice to see you both."

So we had a few nice conversations. Then we didn't. No big deal.

"Hey, Beth." Will's eyes locked onto me. They are cool and casual, unreadable. As is the half-smile that is just begging to be kissed.

He's just playing games.

Jane's locked in a staring contest with Chuck. The look between them has real chemistry—goofy, sweet, unmistakably mutual.

"So," Chuck says, blushing as he locks eyes with Jane. For a second, I half expect him to scuff his toe against the ground and tuck his hands behind his back like a schoolboy, but he manages to stay centered.

Jane beams, because of course she does.

I hesitate. I don't want to walk with them but I can't deny Jane some casual time with Chuck. Can I?

"Uh, we'd love to but I promised Cass I'd help her set up," Jane answers coolly.

Cassie and I both shoot her a look but don't contradict her.

"Yeah, sorry." I say with equal indifference. "Maybe we'll catch up with you guys later." I look pointedly at Will. "Have fun though!" Big smiles.

As they wander off, Cassie pulls Jane close to her and presses, "Okay, what was that about?"

"Nothing," Jane retorts, then looks at me, who I am sure is looking just as baffled. "What? It's girl's night. I'm sticking with the girls!"

"Well played, Wilkes." I put up a knuckled fist for her to bump.

We visit with Cassie for a few more minutes, getting more in the way than helping by any stretch of the imagination. I want to ensure the boys get a good, long head start before we take off on our own boozy adventure.

As Jane and I walk off, arm in arm, I lean into her.

"You wanted to go with Chuck, didn't you?"

"Of course I did." she answers simply, seeming unaffected by the sacrifice.

"And you didn't because…"

"Because what Will did, lying to you about who he was, is a dick move and I didn't want to make you uncomfortable." She squeezes my arm under her own.

"Okay, but next time the opportunity arises, you take that man up on it!" I scold.

"Yes, ma'am," Jane nods and salutes with her wine glass.

"I love you, sister." I say as we continue down the sidewalk.

When we see them a few businesses down the road, we veer, successfully avoiding them for the night. I turn my head away from that whole side of the street, lest I catch a glimpse of fitted pants or that smarmy smile.

Sure, avoidance doesn't solve anything—but it's a hell of a temporary solution.

I sip something dry and floral, laughing as Jane does a dramatic spit take at a too-sweet Riesling. Will and his too-perfect smile fade into the background, just another ripple in the crowd.

Maybe someday I'll deal with all that.

Today, I'm all about wine, sun, and sisterhood.

* * *

Wine Walk

Will

There's Beth, across the street, pretending I don't exist. The second she found out I wasn't just some guy with calluses and a truck, she flipped the switch—flirty to frosty. She probably doesn't like men with money. I've met the type before. They see wealth like a disease. Or maybe she's just still embarrassed from the concert.

Either way, I'd be lying if I said the green sundress and knee-high boots weren't messing with my ability to stay annoyed. She can play it cool all she wants, but the way that belt cinches her waist feels like a dare.

"Isn't that right, Will?"

"Huh?" I blink and turn, finding Chuck mid-sentence. Something about zoning and retaining walls.

"Wow," he says, chuckling. "Riveting stuff, huh?"

"Yeah. Sorry. I got distracted."

He follows my gaze across the street and grins like a jackal. "Ah. That kind of distracted."

"Not even," I lie, straightening the wine glass in my hand like it'll give me something better to do than keep glancing in her direction.

David, another local Chuck introduced me to, smirks. "That's a pretty hot distraction. You two got history?"

"Just a couple of conversations." I shrug. "It's complicated."

"It always is."

We keep walking, weaving through the crowd. Chuck greets what feels like half the town, shaking hands and clapping backs like he's running for office. I smile and converse well enough, but my attention keeps flickering to Beth—especially when she starts laughing at something the older woman next to her says.

She's waving her wine glass dramatically, hair bouncing in the breeze, laughing like the whole damn world is in on the joke.

She's magnetic.

Jane's next to her, just as charming, if a little more reserved. Chuck's already gone starry-eyed. I'm not sure which one of us is in deeper.

David nudges me. "If you're not gonna introduce me to Beth, think Jane would?"

"Nope." My answer is immediate and probably too sharp. He lifts an eyebrow but doesn't push.

We keep moving. As we pass a local pottery booth, I pause. There's a wide ceramic bowl—earthy, uneven in shape, glazed in dusty turquoise. It's handmade. The artist is leaning back in his canvas chair, holding a brush up to a cup demonstrating a technique to a starry eyed kid.

"This is an underglaze, it goes on before the first fire."

I pick up the bowl and turn it over in my hands. It's imperfect and beautiful, clearly formed by someone who gives a damn.

"You like that one?" the potter asks—a wiry man in his sixties with hands like driftwood and a tattoo of a hawk just visible under his rolled sleeve.

"I do."

"That one's handmade. If you like symmetry, these over here are thrown on the wheel for an even rim. I like making those out of an imbalanced or ruined throw. Rather than recycling the clay, I just turn it into whatever it wants to be." He holds up a similar piece with reverence, as though it made itself.

"The work is beautiful. How much for a set of those smaller bowls and this one here?"

He considers each and gives me a total. I hand him cash and shake his hand firmly. "You got a card?"

He hands it over. "I do custom pieces too, if you ever need 'em. Dinnerware sets, teapots and mugs. I even dabble in sculpture when the mood strikes."

I thank him and pocket it. I don't know what I'll use the large, misshapen bowl for. Might just leave it empty on a table. But something about it feels honest. Like it belongs.

Chuck gives me a curious look as I rejoin the group. "Didn't know you were into pottery."

"I'm into craftsmanship," I reply. "Might come in handy for the ranch later."

He shrugs, satisfied.

Down the road, someone's dropped a trail of flyers—probably from the wind. I stoop to pick them up, stacking them neatly on a nearby table. No one notices, and I'm not looking for praise. It just needs to be done.

As I straighten the pile, my phone buzzes in my pocket. I slip it out, expecting it to be Gia sending a selfie with one of the goats.

It's Aunt Cathy.

Subject: Financial Disbursement Restrictions

William,

I've reviewed your recent inquiries. As you were reminded last quarter, family funds will not be made available for this endeavor. If you insist on continuing this... experiment... you'll need to rely on the pittance left you by your wayward father. I trust you will act accordingly.

Catherine Fitzgerald

Executive Trustee - Fitzgerald Family Holdings

I read it twice. Three times.

Curt. Clinical. Somehow still condescending. In other words, exactly what I've come to expect from Aunt Cathy.

I slide the phone back into my pocket before anyone notices.

The wine in my glass suddenly tastes bitter. I glance around the tent—the lights, the music, the easy laughter. Gia would love this vibe. Had I known a wine walk could be this family-friendly, I might've brought her along.

But right now, all I see are busted fences, unopened invoices, and Cathy's words burned behind my eyes. It's best Gia didn't come. She doesn't need to deal with this part of the business. Not yet, anyway.

Wayward father. Pittance.

My jaw clenches. I force myself to exhale, to relax my grip on the glass, to plaster the same damn polite smile I've been wearing since I got here.

Beth is talking to one of the vendors now—animated, passionate, beautiful. I want to be here. I want this to work. But for the first time since I signed those papers, I wonder if I made a mistake.

Maybe I need to flip the place. Just cut my losses and get Gia back to the city.

I smile again. Pretend it's fine.

I glance toward Beth's side of the street—but she's gone. It's probably for the best. I think straighter when she's not around.

If I'm going to figure out what to do, I need all the focus I can muster. And if Beth Wilkes has one fatal flaw, it's that she already has *too much* of my focus.

Sixteen

Barbecued

Beth

"We're here!" I announce boisterously, contending with the cacophony of murmured conversation already filling the empty space of a rather large entry way.

"Beth?" I hear from what I assume is the kitchen. "Jane?"

"Yep, it's us!" I shout as Jane shushes me.

"You're being rude!" She chides.

"I'm announcing our presence," I explain then shout, "Shoes or no shoes?"

Jane cringes but Chuck returns with, "Shoes are fine! Come on in!"

We follow the sound through an archway that opens up into a massive kitchen adorned with solid cherry wood cabinets and dark marble counter tops. Inside stands Chuck and a couple of guys I don't recognize. No Will.

I exhale in relief. Then, for reasons I refuse to examine, I feel an unexpected flicker of disappointment.

Chuck grins. "I'm glad you two could make it!" Still holding the whiskey bottle he was about to open, he pulls me into a quick, friendly hug. Then he turns to Jane.

"Hey, Jane." His voice softens.

I watch, rapt with amusement, as they do the awkward hug dance.

Step forward—same direction—oh no, almost a nose bump—now a hesitant correction—

Finally, they manage a full embrace, lingering just a second too long for a strictly platonic hug.

One day they're going to make the most beautiful babies. I smirk at my own secret joke.

Chuck throws an arm over Jane's shoulder and gestures toward the kitchen. "Beth, Jane—this is Terry and his partner Mike."

The two men raise their drinks in our direction. Terry is burly with a red beard, Mike looks relaxed and sun-bronzed—both sound totally West Coast.

Chuck continues, rattling off names from the living room. I catch a Sam (probably short for Samantha), a Derek (who I think is with Megan), and a Jake (or is it John?).

I smile, nod, and promptly forget half of them.

After introductions Chuck offers us drinks. We both decline the Whiskey and sift through the proffered ice chest for beers.

"Anyway, ladies—I was just telling Mike and Terry about the worst client of my life. Where was I? Oh yeah—so, after months of nonsense, this guy suddenly wants to close two weeks early—and take fifty grand off his own asking price!"

The four of us do a combination of incredulous laughter and harrumphing, fueling him to continue. "Anyway, I'm his agent, right, not his mommy, so I gotta do what he asks. I draw up the addendum, which I think is horse shit by the way, and send it over to the seller's agent. And let me tell you, I was so thankful the seller pulled out." Terry put his arms up in the air in a silent hallelujah as Chuck continued, "I mean she hung in there for *three months* of this guy's antics and was such a sport but he clearly poured lemon juice on all those wounds he'd been inflicting."

"Ah, man! Good for her. Weren't you bummed you lost the commission?" Terry asks, sipping his pinot.

Chuck holds his hands out as though he's about to say 'ehhh, maybe,' but Terry's partner, Mike, adds, "Yeah, how much were they selling the estate for? Like a cool three mil? What's fifty thousand less? And you would have made a killer profit!" Both men have California surfer-boy accents I find endearing, having just returned from the Bay myself.

"Honestly, I was weelin' and dealin' so hard in those days I didn't mind. I think the seller ultimately made the right choice. She sold it within a month for over asking price." Chuck shrugs and pours Mike a drink from what looks like a very expensive bottle of whiskey.

I'm impressed by his response.

"A man of principle," Jane says softly, "I like that."

"Thanks," Chuck blushes, "But don't give me too much credit. I was so done with the prick myself I was willing to give up the commission just to be free of him."

Oh, Chuck, take the damn compliment, would you? As I laugh inwardly at their awkward courting dance, my head turns, and I catch a glimpse of Will across the room, leaning casually against the wall, whiskey glass in hand, immersed in conversation.

My stomach drops. *What the hell? Where did he even come from?*

Part of me thought he was avoiding me. I was almost… flattered? But nope. That's not it. Turns out, I'm not even on his radar.

For a second—just one stupid second—I feel the heat of that coffee shop smile. The easy charm. The way he'd listened. Then I remember the concert. His smirk. His dismissal. His arrogance.

I inhale sharply, straightening my spine, and forcing my shoulders back. *No. Not again. Not tonight.*

I'm not at the dinner party for him. I'm there for Jane. She had been invited by Chuck and didn't want to go alone to a party where she didn't know anyone. It's a small town, yes, but he's a big-timey, whiskey drinking real estate agent and she teaches dance to five year olds at a local dance studio and attends a monthly book club at Luminary. They don't exactly run in the same circles. I am happy to come on her behalf, and I'm genuinely enjoying myself. There is no way I'm going to let Will get to me. Again.

Sunrises and Sagebrush

* * *

Drinks poured and stories told, the crowd moves outside to gather around the fire pit while Chuck mans the barbecue. The smell of meats in the smoker make whatever he's about to toss onto the grill go up a thousand percent in my estimation.

"Can I help with anything?" I ask as he fires up the propane and I eye the tray of smoked sausages and marinated rib eyes. My mouth waters just looking at the raw slabs.

"Absolutely! In the fridge in the garage there's a big aluminum tray with skewered veggies."

"On it." I don't know where his garage is, but I'm feeling adventurous so I don't ask. That, and Will is playing cornhole with the Jake guy so I'm happy to busy myself in another direction.

The garage is easy to find, once I determine that the other end of the house is full of bedrooms, one of which is set up as an office and another as a guest room- not that I go snooping or anything.

I pull out the massive tin of veggie kabobs. Between the appetizers and sides already sprawled across the kitchen counter and the plethora of meats outside, the skewers would have seemed unnecessary except that I love grilled mushrooms and onions and, was that pineapple? Yeah, I'm down. If I die of a heart attack tonight, I'm going to die happy.

I practically skip my way back through the kitchen onto the backyard patio—and then pull up short. I frown. Standing in his place at the barbecue is none other than the million-dollar man. I look around for Chuck only to find him across the yard playing bocce ball with Jane.

Alright, Beth, you can do this.

"Hey, Will," I say, way more weakly than I intend.

He glances sideways at me and replies, "Oh, hey."

"Yeah, uh, Chuck asked for these. I can just, uh, set them down here, if you'd like." Inwardly, I toss a bucket of cold water over my face, trying to reboot the system as I'm clearly glitching.

He adds the last of the ribeyes, closing the barbecue before the cool air eats away all the heat. The sausages are still waiting for their turn on the platter. Had he just thrown them on with the steaks, they would've overcooked.

Color me impressed.

"Actually," he says as I turn to leave, "with this many skewers, I could use your help."

The last thing I want to do is stand by this man and help him cook. Can't he charm some other woman into it? Or get one of Chuck's barbecue-beer-buds to step in?

"Yeah, okay. Sure."

Will tilts his head, considering me. "You know your way around a barbecue?"

It doesn't sound like a challenge. But I take it as one anyway.

"I think I can manage," I say coolly. "Can you?"

He chuckles, glances at his watch, then crosses his arms. His forearms flex—stupid, strong forearms that should not make my pulse do a thing. But they do.

Focus, Beth. It's going to be the mantra of the night.

"We'll find out, won't we?" he murmurs, and the daring challenge in his voice makes me want to smack the smug right off his face.

Or kiss it off.

Hell, I don't know which.

"I'm going to grab another drink real quick. You want anything?"

"I'll take whatever you're having."

"I didn't know someone with such refined tastes would care for anything less than a finely aged brandy." I cringe. Am I being mean just to be mean? Is this my version of flirting?

He puts on a pretentious British accent. "Ah, yes, well I typically prefer a good Bowmore, but given that I find myself inexplicably fraternizing among commoners such as yourself, I shall endeavor to imbibe in the customary drink, however unrefined. When in Rome, as they say." He waves his hand in mock conceit, but there's an unmistakable edge of annoyance in his sarcasm.

I deserve that. I bow with a flourish and go to grab us a couple of drinks. Coke for me, Bud Light for the prince. He drinks it without complaint, even seems to enjoy it.

As he flips the steak, I help him load fifty million vegetable kabobs onto the grill, arranging as many as I can around the plump, darkening steaks. We work in silence—him on the meats, me on the veggies—until all is cooked and plattered. We each carry the fruits of our labor into the kitchen, where Chuck is entertaining a well-dressed couple, Jane smiling sweetly at his side. He's been busy with the smoked meats, which are now appropriately cut, chopped, or pulled and piled in heaps across the center of the massive island counter.

"Wow! That looks delicious!" Jane and Chuck both exclaim, then laugh.

Chuck thanks us for handling the barbecue and helps us add the trays to the smorgasbord.

Then it's speech time—thank you all for coming, a quick rundown of the food and games, and then we're off to the races, piling our plates.

Everything looks so good, I load mine with more than I can possibly eat. When Will remarks that he's never seen a woman with such a voracious appetite, I smirk and toss another smoked rib across the top of my potato salad.

I spend the better part of the evening eating, chatting, and getting my ass kicked at cornhole. I'm in my element. It feels good, like being back to my roots. As I step back from the wooden ramp, I feel a presence come up behind me.

"Oops! Sorry," I start to say as I turn.

"Care to go another round?" Will's voice is silky smooth.

I glance around, desperate for an escape. Jake—yes, Jake!—has just beaten me again and moved off to check in with his buds. Jane is fully engrossed in a conversation with Chuck, both lounging by the fire pit. His arm is up over the bench behind her. She is going to be no help whatsoever.

As though it's the answer to my problem, I say, "I really suck at cornhole."

Will bends down and starts picking up bean bags. "Good. So do I."

I huff and make my way to the other end of the lawn, where the second inclined board sits, speckled with the bean bags I've flung.

He seems relaxed as we play, and I start to think maybe the animosity is calming down. He's easygoing, can cook a mean steak, and is, in fact, trash at cornhole. I laugh as we alternate tossing bean bags—some fall short, some go long, some bounce right over the hole.

"Yes!" I jump and dance as one of mine finally drops in.

"Not bad!" Will cheers. "You may yet reach tournament levels after all."

"Pretty sure it went in by accident," I concede, and we both laugh.

Whoa. We both laugh. And not at the other's expense. I'm starting to feel like maybe he's alright. Not datable, what with a girlfriend and all, but I can be friends with him. Can't I?

We start our third game, which is going equally dismally—until I make my second toss, and he nails his. I miss my third. He nails his again. Then his fourth goes in.

"Wow! Lucky throws." I grin. "Did you just find your zone or something?"

Will shrugs, all nonchalant.

Then—Chuck claps him on the back. "Oh man, remember college? This guy cleaned everyone out. Couldn't beat him if you tried."

My stomach twists.

Are you kidding me?

My fingers tighten around the bean bags. I glance at Will, expecting a guilty look, a sheepish grin—something.

Nothing. Just that same, charming, innocent expression.

My anger snaps. Just when I think this guy might not be so bad, he one-ups himself.

I smile at Chuck and say something about not minding—cornhole's not really my game anyway. I gather up the bags and pile them neatly beside the board.

"You done?" Chuck calls. "Just as we were coming to watch!"

"Or I'll play with you," Jane appears beside him and takes his hand.

Good for them, I think sincerely, but the sentiment feels sour in my mouth.

"Yeah, I'm all tossed out. Gotta take a break. It's all yours if you two want to play." I head across the grass toward the house. As I pass Will, I whisper, "asshole," and keep going.

I get down the hall, halfway to the bathroom where I fully intend to sit and fume for a good ten minutes, when I feel a hand on my shoulder.

"Hey," Will spits. "What's wrong with you?"

I turn, glaring. "What's wrong with me, 'Bill'? Gee, I don't know. Being lied to and manipulated just rubs a girl the wrong way, you know. Or maybe you're used to your women liking that, *Bill*. I mean seriously, what even was that all about anyway?"

"What are you talking about? You made it clear you didn't like the owner of the ranch. You expect me to own right up to it?" Will's voice rises in frustration.

"Yes! Dammit! At the coffee shop I thought you were genuinely sweet and, I don't know, the whole 'new cowboy in town' act was awkward and endearing, but that's not who you really are, is it? Oh! And you said your name was 'Bill.' What even was that?"

"William, Will, Bill—what does it matter? I didn't lie. You were the one getting flirty with the version of me you liked, while tearing down who I actually am. And out there? You're getting all worked up 'cause I threw a few games? I didn't want you to feel bad—"

"How chivalrous!" I cut in, turning to storm off.

He follows closely behind. "So I'm a bad guy for trying to relate to you? Come on, that's not fair."

I spin, pinning him to the wall. "Fair? What do you know about fair? You get to make up all the rules in your world, just do what you want, consequences be—"

He steps closer, and suddenly, it's my back against the wall.

My breath stutters.

He's so damn close. I can feel the warmth of him, the way his chest rises and falls too fast, like he's just as furious as I am. Just as undone.

"You think you know everything about me," he murmurs, voice low. "But you don't know a damn thing, Beth."

Silence pulses between us.

And then—like we both snap at the same time—I grab his collar and crash my mouth into his.

I'd like to say this is where my logic kicks back in and I push him away, but that's not what happens.

Seventeen

Oh, Right...

Beth

Our bodies barely part, coming up for air only when absolutely necessary. His hands roam my torso, searching, discovering, claiming. I don't resist. My fingers find the crisp hem of his shirt, slipping between fabric and skin until I reach the heat of his stomach, feeling the taut muscles beneath.

God. He feels like an athlete.

"What do you do to me?" he murmurs between kisses, his lips trailing fire from my mouth down to my neck.

I gasp as he finds the spot—the one that turns my knees weak.

"Hell if I know," I whisper, my voice wrecked.

Voices drift from the kitchen. A reminder. We're not exactly alone.

I grip his belt and move, backing us up, searching for anywhere that offers privacy. He follows seamlessly, pressing against me, every step tangled in heat and friction until—the first door.

I don't even care if it's an office or a closet. But when the backs of my legs hit a mattress, I exhale.

Bedroom it is.

My hands work at his shirt buttons, fumbling in my urgency. He yanks my blouse over my head in one fluid motion, eyes darkening when he sees my pink lace bra. I wore it because it's comfortable. But the way he looks at me?

It's like I wore it just for him.

"You're beautiful," he murmurs, his gaze devouring everything—every inch, every curve.

I bite my lip as he kisses my stomach, his lips brushing reverent paths down my skin.

"So are you," I laugh breathily, my fingers threading through his hair.

I should be thinking. I should remember who he is—what he represents. But the only voice in my head right now is screaming for more. Which he seems all too happy to deliver.

His hands slide behind me, expertly unclasping my bra. The lace slips away, tossed into the abyss. Then—his mouth closes around my nipple. A jolt of pure, unfiltered pleasure shoots through me.

"Shit," I exhale, digging my fingers into his shoulders as he sucks, nips, and teases.

My hands tear at his shirt buttons, desperate, frantic—until he rips the last one clean off. His shirt's gone, discarded, and he doesn't stop to care.

My fingers slide past his belt, diving lower, slipping beneath his waistband until I find his cock.

He groans loudly as I wrap my fingers around it.

"Shhh," I grin against his lips, tightening my grip. "We have to be quiet."

"Right," he growls, breath hitching. "Wouldn't want anyone to know what we're doing in here."

Then his hands are on my leggings, sliding them down, down, over my ankles. I barely have time to react before he's pushing me back, dropping to his knees between my legs. His mouth finds me.

His tongue is unbearable. Too good. Too much. Every slow, devastating stroke sends me spiraling, and it's not long before I'm trembling, clutching at the sheets, whispering his name like a prayer.

"Fucking hell," I pant, trying not to cry out.

He doesn't stop. Doesn't relent. He keeps working me over until I'm turning my face into the pillow to stop the orgasm from alerting the rest of the party.

And that's just the beginning.

He pulls his pants and boxer briefs off, exposing one of the most beautiful cocks I've ever seen—if not *the* most beautiful. I take hold of it with one hand and guide him onto the bed with the other.

"Condom," I think I say as I lower my mouth onto him, taking him as deeply as I can. He tastes like heaven.

"Wha?" he breathes between low, barely contained moans.

I play with him for a few more seconds before coming up for air. "Do you have a condom?"

"Fuck. No, I don't." His head drops heavily back on the pillow. "Do you?"

"No," I growl.

I reach over and open the drawers of the bedside table. Tissues, various toiletries... I search frantically, hoping Chuck is sex-positive and doesn't mind people—bingo! I pull out a line of three condoms and tear at the perforation to remove one. I don't have time to consider whether Chuck is a player or just responsible. Right now I only have one man on my mind and I need him inside of me.

"You're a fucking goddess," he says and pulls me on top of him, worshipping my tongue with his own. I feel him hard between my legs as his hips begin to move. I'm tempted to let him push into me right then, skin against skin.

"Wait. One sec," I breathe as I lift myself up, straddling him with his hard cock just in front of me.

I tear open the condom and slide it down onto him. He moans again as I run my other hand down his length. Thankfully, it's a good fit.

I climb on top of him and if either of us had any inhibitions left, they flee fast. No words pass between us, only moaning (which we do our best to keep quiet), breathing, and touching.

So much touching.

One condom down. One orgasm each. Still not enough.

He kisses me like he'll never stop, like I'm the only thing he's ever wanted. And maybe, for tonight, that's true.

Oh, Right...

We don't stop at one.

By the time we're spent and tangled, the row of three are used up. My body hums with satisfaction, my skin slick with sweat, and I don't care about anything except the way his arms feel around me.

He kisses me again—soft, slow, lingering. The kind of kiss that says something.

"You are incredible," he whispers.

"So are you," I murmur, barely able to form words.

He exhales deeply, content, satisfied.

Then—he checks his phone.

And just like that, everything changes. His body tenses and his expression shifts.

"Shit. It's later than I thought." He sits up quickly, running a hand through his messy hair.

I frown, warmth curdling into unease. "Is everything okay?"

"Yeah. Yeah, it's fine," he says, but the passion is gone. The intimacy replaced by something else. Something colder.

Worry? Or shame?

"I just told Gia I'd be home early." He stands, pulling on his boxers and slacks. "She's probably worried. I should get going."

I feel like I've just been punched in the gut.

Right. Gia. His girlfriend.

I sit there, stunned. Blindsided. How could I have forgotten?

You were just a distraction. A side piece. First I was the one being cheated on, now I am the one being cheated *with*. The feeling of that realization is like burning coal in my belly.

I swallow, forcing my voice light, detached. "Yeah. You should do that."

He's too busy buttoning his ruined shirt to notice the way my smile falters, or how my hands suddenly feel like dead weight in my lap.

I force my body into motion, grabbing my blouse, untangling it from the sheets.

Will must feel the shift in the air, because suddenly, he turns back.

"Hey." He reaches for my hands, stopping me mid-motion. "I'm sorry to rush out like this. It's not about you, I promise." He hesitates. "I just—this wasn't—"

He trails off, expression conflicted.

How cute. The playboy is at a loss for words.

Don't let him see it hurts.

I smile. Easy. Dismissive. "Yeah, yeah. No worries. I get it. It's not like we planned this."

His relief is instant. "Right! Thank you for understanding. You really are incredible."

"Nah, it's nothing," I say, my voice too light, too empty.

He peeks into the hallway, making sure it's clear before slipping out. And just like that—he's gone.

I sit there for another minute, staring at the empty doorway, at the tangle of sheets.

Nothing. That's all this was. A momentary lapse in judgment—one that absolutely will never happen again.

Eighteen

The Morning After

Will

I pour the last glob of viscous white goop onto the stove top griddle. It hisses as it spreads into a circle across the surface. The smell of bacon and pancakes fills the house—better than any candle. I feel light and energized, despite a restless night.

A smirk tugs at my lips as I remember the feel of Beth against me.

Gia stands at the center island, intently mashing strawberries and scooping the mush into a test tube filled with clear liquid. The counter's a disaster—papers, her laptop, bowls, bottles, and the now-empty plastic container that once held strawberries are spread everywhere.

Leaning over her plate of syrup-drenched pancakes and three slices of bacon, Gia shoves a dripping bite into her mouth while she works. It's her second plate. I have no idea where she puts it all. The image reminds me of what I said to Beth last night about her filled plate. Gia's nothing like most girls I know. But then, neither is Beth.

Gia grabs a strawberry from the pile, dips it in syrup, and pops it into her mouth.

I shake my head, smiling.

"You're not supposed to eat your science experiment," I tease.

"Sure I am!" she fires back. She holds up a test tube filled with strawberry mush and clear liquid. "Want some?"

I flip a pancake and glance over at her mad science setup. I pick up the test tube and slosh it around. Online school to finish out the semester means in-kitchen science. Fun.

"What's in this again?"

Gia shrugs. "Oh, you know, strawberries, dish soap, and rubbing alcohol."

She laughs as I scrunch my nose and hand it back. I return to flipping duty, finishing up a batch of batter that turned out way bigger than either of us can eat in one sitting.

As Gia plays mad scientist and I pour the last of the batter, my thoughts drift—Beth's kiss in the hallway, the feel of her skin against mine. I shudder, then shake it off. Pancakes. Little sister. Focus. But damn, that lingering feeling is a good one.

I pull out my phone and type.

Last night was sexy. So are you.

Short. Simple. Just the right amount of flirty. I hit send and stare at the screen, caught in the warm afterglow of last night—until something pulls me back.

A sniffing sound from behind.

"Are you burning something?"

Gia's voice snaps me fully back. I look down. The final pancake is smoking angrily on the griddle.

"Oops!" I laugh. "Guess this last one didn't make it."

I toss the half-charred, half-raw thing in the trash and twist the dial on the griddle.

"Mom used to make the best pancakes." Gia looks up from her experiment, her eyes losing focus.

My chest tightens. "She sure did, Gigi. I'll just have to keep working on mine."

"They'll never be as good," she says matter-of-factly. But her mouth twitches, and a hint of a smile creeps in.

"No, not even close. But they make a good tribute, don't they?" I hold one up with a fork. It sags down around it like a lazy sombrero.

That makes Gia laugh. "Definitely!"

I fix myself a plate of syrupy pancakes with a side of heart attack and dig in. Gia says something but I am on my phone, scrolling absentmindedly.

"You seem distracted," Gia says, still focused on the test tube as she carefully inserts a cotton swab into the mixture.

"Yeah, sorry." I don't offer more.

"Is it that Beth girl you've been gushing over?" She raises an eyebrow behind the oversized safety glasses she's clearly only wearing for dramatic effect.

None of your business, I want to say. But before I can answer, Gia explodes with joy.

"Eeee! Look! DNA! I made my own DNA!"

Her grin stretches ear to ear as she holds the cotton swab above the test tube. A string of white, mucus-like goo hangs from it.

"My sister, the scientist." I grin back, even though I have no idea how that booger on a stick is DNA.

I lean into the distraction, grateful for it. The bacon is crispy perfection. The woman who once called me the enemy practically melted in my hands last night. My sister's conquering the universe, one strawberry at a time. Life is good.

I clear my plate while Gia scribbles in her notes.

"I'm heading out to work in the yard," I tell her.

"Yep!" she chirps, tongue poking out as she writes on an index card.

"If you need any help, come grab me, okay?" I back up a little, hoping maybe she'll ask me to stay.

"Mmm-hhmmm." She barely registers me, totally absorbed in her project.

I head down the stairs off the laundry room, feeling light on my feet. As I reach the bottom, I pull out my phone and check for a reply.

Nothing.

But I'm not worried. Beth's probably knee-deep in clients already. I gotta hand it to her, that girl's got drive. It's time to get back to work. Ben's guys

will be here to help with the stall any minute.
Now... Where the hell is that post-hole digger?

Nineteen

No Big Deal

Beth

The first thing I see when my eyes blink open is the popcorn ceiling of my childhood bedroom. As it comes into focus, so does last night's blunder. A crushing feeling presses against my chest. I silence my alarm clock and lie there, staring at the peaks and valleys, noting the dusty cobwebs stretched across the corner of the ceiling. This is what my life has come to.

Quit it, Beth. You're only thirty-two.

I *feel* twice that. Or half, judging by my recent lapse in judgment.

I know better. I'm not a child. Learn, move on.

It's just the pep-scolding I need. Horse therapy—that's what brought me back home. I mean, besides family. I just need to refocus. I don't need a man clouding my judgment or taking my eyes off the prize. I've got website tweaks to make, a meeting with Carol at eleven, and a couple of late afternoon clients to round out the day.

But first—shower.

I let the hot droplets and freesia bubbles wash the funk off my body and out of my soul. I take my time luxuriating. When the bubbles remind me of his touch, I remind myself it was just a fantasy. When my stomach flips remembering his lips on mine, I swap the image for one of a hound dog slinking home to his girlfriend, tail between his legs. The mental picture makes me laugh.

Pathetic.

By the time I'm done, I feel better. Body, mind, and soul. Cleansed of my silly crush and ready to slay.

With a cup of fresh coffee and some avocado toast, I open my laptop.

-Pa-ting!-

My phone lights up with a new message.

I glance down, still smiling from my productive energy.

Last night was so sexy. So are you.

You know that gif of the woman coughing up her coffee with laughter? That's me, in real time, as coffee sprays across the screen of my laptop.

"Oh, shit!" I toss my phone aside and scramble for a napkin, dabbing sugar and caffeine off my poor, innocent MacBook.

I don't pick the phone back up. Not right now. There's a whole laundry list of things I need to do today—and replying to Will is not one of them. By the time I leave for Carol's, I've rewritten my bio (new me, new bio) and played with the formatting on my homepage to exchange city sleek with a warmer, more Western vibe. Two things down from a two-dozen-item to-do list. Not bad for one morning.

I put on a podcast for the twenty-minute drive out to see my mentor and soon-to-be predecessor. The hosts chatter on while the satisfying crunch of gravel beneath my tires signals my arrival.

Carol's property is largely undeveloped. From the street, it looks like a stretch of high desert—sagebrush blanketing the landscape, giving no hint of the manicured horse trails winding quietly through it. Stalls and corrals stretch out from two main structures: her modest, ranch-style home with a wide front porch that doubles as the business office, and a wooden stable built for function over flash. The barn is all charm and practicality—rough-hewn beams, roomy open-air stalls, and the soft scent of hay lingering in the air. It's the kind of place where both horses and humans can breathe a little easier.

I've been working with Carol for a few weeks now, getting ready to take over. I shadowed her with several clients who gave permission, and next week, I'm flying solo. Today, we're diving into the "fun stuff"—taxes and licensing.

"Make sure you maintain this spreadsheet every week," Carol says as she walks me through her system. "Otherwise, you're in for a world of hurt come tax season."

Translation: she does everything old school.

"I'm tellin' ya," she adds with a deadly serious look, "I've done it myself more than once. It's a real kick in the pants."

"Absolutely," I say, meaning it. The minute this business is mine, I'm upgrading to digital systems and automating everything from billing to expense tracking.

This isn't my first rodeo. It is, however, my first time incorporating horses.

After we've gone cross-eyed from spreadsheets, we head out to the stalls. I need more face time with her equine business partners anyway.

"Seems to me you've got the people part down pat," Carol says as we brush one of the horses. "I loved the way you worked with that boy last week—Matty. He's been through a real rough patch, and most of his teachers have written him off as defiant. He hasn't opened up much to me, but he responded to you. That gives me hope."

"Thank you." I smile, letting it sink in.

"But don't forget," she adds, her voice turning gruff, "it's not just about the people. These animals need care too. If you don't put just as much energy into *them*—maybe more—you'll never make it in this field."

I like Carol. She's got that tough-love, no-nonsense grandma energy I didn't know I needed.

"Oh, for sure. I mean, I won't be scooping up a client's poop, for one thing," I joke.

She narrows her eyes like she might scold me—then bursts out laughing.

"See? I knew you were the right one to take over for me." Her laugh echoes down the line of stalls as we move from horse to horse, giving each some individual attention.

Two of the four horses will stay with me. The other two are retiring alongside Carol. I give "my" two a little extra time.

"How's Gypsy doing?" she asks while we nuzzle and sweet-talk the fur babies.

"Good! I think she's going to make a wonderful therapy horse. She's still young enough to train properly and so sweet-natured. I didn't realize how meticulous the certification process would be for me, but I've got high hopes for her."

"Meh," she brushes off my concerns, "Just stay consistent with training. That's the key."

"Yup." I say as I rub my hand down Cocoa's nose.

Consistency, not just in work but in life. *That's* the key.

Twenty

Progress

Beth

Consistency is exactly what I focus on when I return the next day, ready to guide and be guided.

The sun peeks over the mountains like it's still waking up, casting long golden rays across the ranch. The air smells like alfalfa and dust, with the faintest hint of morning manure—so basically, it smells like home. My boots crunch softly against the gravel as I cross Carol's yard, headed for the small paddock on the east side.

Birdsong filters through the trees. Somewhere in the distance, a horse snorts. It's calm. Settling. Exactly what I need before my first solo run—well, supervised solo. Carol's watching from the shadows, clipboard in hand, ready to jump in if needed but letting me take the reins.

Literally.

Today's client is Cody. He's twelve years old. He was referred by the school after a fight with a classmate and an escalating string of "behavioral issues." Angry, oppositional. Carol said he's not great with adults. He's even worse with silence. But animals? That's where we might get somewhere.

I spot him at the fence, arms crossed, scowl firmly in place like he's daring the world to fight him first. He's smaller than I thought he'd be. His jeans are too long, his hoodie is shredded at the cuffs, and his hair looks like he combed it with a leaf blower.

So basically: a preteen.

"Cody?" I ask as I approach with a slow, even gait. "Hey. I'm Beth."

He glances up, but doesn't say anything.

I resist the urge to fill the silence. Instead, I point to the corral. "This is Hazel. She's a good listener. She doesn't say much, but she's curious about you."

He eyes the horse, eyes me, then shrugs.

Progress.

"Want to help me brush her?" I keep my tone light, casual.

Another shrug. Then, slowly, he steps forward.

I hand him the brush and demonstrate long, slow strokes along Hazel's flank. He mirrors me with more pressure than finesse, but I'm not picky.

"You ever worked with horses before?" I ask.

"Nope."

"Well, you're doing just fine." I don't push. Just work beside him, two people sharing a moment without needing to fill it with noise. I let the silence stretch until the weight of it shifts from awkward to peaceful.

"Hazel's a mustang. Rescued. Took a while for her to trust people again."

Cody pauses in his brushing.

I don't explain. I just let the words hang there like bait.

"She don't look scared," he finally mutters.

"She's not. Not anymore."

He goes quiet again, brushing more carefully now.

"Wanna walk her?" I ask, nodding to the lead rope coiled nearby.

Another beat. Then he nods.

I guide him through the process—how to hold the rope, how to keep her close without crowding her space. Hazel follows his lead with surprising grace. I can see Cody's shoulders shift—relaxing just a hair.

"You're doing good," I say. "Steady hands."

He doesn't respond, but I catch the ghost of a smirk.

After a few loops, we pause by the fence. I guide him through a grounding exercise: both hands on Hazel's shoulder, feet flat on the earth.

"Feel her breathing?" I say. When he shrugs I add, "Try to match it."

Cody exhales, rough at first. Then again. Slower. Deeper. It's a good start.

Afterward, we remove the lead rope together. He winds it up without being asked. He doesn't bolt when it's over. He lingers. That's how I know it mattered.

"Same time next week?" I ask.

He shrugs. "I guess."

I'll take it.

When his ride pulls up—an aunt, judging by the impatient honk—he gives Hazel one last pat and trudges off. I watch until the truck kicks up a cloud of dust down the drive.

I let out a breath I didn't realize I was holding.

Carol appears beside me, sipping from a battered enamel mug that says Ranch Life is Best Life. She raises an eyebrow.

"You didn't scare him off," she says.

"Not yet."

She places a hand on my shoulder. "You were steady. Present. Consistent."

"Trying," I murmur, and I mean it.

She nods toward the stables. "Cocoa could use a stretch and clean-up."

I wave a hand in mock salute. "On it."

The stalls smell like old hay and warm fur—comforting, earthy. I lean into the task, brushing Cocoa's coat with long, even strokes. He exhales slowly, shifting his weight beneath me.

"Yeah," I whisper. "Me too."

I think about Cody. About how every kid seems to carry something sharp under their skin. How sometimes they need a gentle place to let it out. I think about consistency again—how Carol keeps reminding me that showing up matters just as much as saying the right thing.

The buzz in my back pocket breaks the rhythm.

I pull out my phone, expecting a calendar reminder or a text from Jane. Instead, it's Will.

Still thinking about last night. Any chance you're free this afternoon?

I stare at the screen.

A moment passes. Then another.

Cocoa nudges my side with his nose.

I reach up and scratch his forehead. "Yeah, I know."

I don't answer the text. But I don't put the phone away either.

Twenty-One

The Anniversary

Will

I glance over at Gia, who's supposed to be helping me stake out rows for the vegetable garden. We're standing in the middle of the flat dirt patch Ben cleared last week. The dozer's still going across the property, pushing through another wall of sagebrush with that steady grind of metal and earth.

Gia's not helping. She's just standing there, staring at her phone. I'm pretty sure she hasn't even moved in a minute. Her face is unreadable.

I blow out a breath and wipe sweat off my forehead with my sleeve. "Gia, for the love of God, if you're not going to help, can you at least hand me the hammer?"

Her head snaps up, blinking like I yanked her out of a trance. "What? I'm just taking a break."

"With one stake in and me standing here holding the next one up?"

"I didn't say you had to help me," she mutters. "I don't even get why this needs to be done right now."

"You want a ranch, right?"

"Yeah, but why do we need to work right *now*? Why gardening?"

I grit my teeth. "We've been through this. The whole ranch—your ranch—

is a full experience, remember? Guests, tours, fresh eggs, fresh vegetables. You said you wanted this."

She shrugs. "I didn't say I wanted to sweat to death planting carrots in the desert."

I shake my head. "This was all your idea."

She throws her arms out. "Sure, but, like, you never ask what I want to do, or when. You come up with the plans and I just have to follow your orders."

I drop the stake and turn to her, trying to keep my tone light. "I've been busting my ass trying to make your dream happen, Gia. I'm building this for you."

"Well, maybe I don't want it anymore!" she yells, voice cracking.

The hammer dangles from her fingers before she lets it drop into the dirt and storms off toward the house.

I stand there for a second, stunned. The air feels hotter now, thick with frustration. Kids make no sense. It's my job to take care of her and guess what the fuck is wrong with her. And I'm coming up dry. I let the stake fall from my hand and follow her inside.

By the time I hit the screen door, I hear the slam of her bedroom door.

I rub both hands over my face and lean on the counter. What the hell just happened? She was excited this morning. She made pancakes. Talked about paint colors for the guest houses. Now this? Women have unpredictable emotions, I can respect that. But this feels outta left field.

I pull out my phone and stare at the blank screen. Beth. Maybe she'll know what to say. I hit her contact. It rings once before going to voicemail.

"Hey. It's Will. I know you haven't gotten back to me… and I'm not trying to make things complicated, but it's Gia. She's really not okay, and I don't know what to do. If you can text or call, I'd appreciate it."

I hate leaving messages but that one felt particularly awkward. Supposing I'm on my own for this one, I head to Gia's room.

"Gia, come on. What's going on?" I knock.

"Stop pretending like you don't know!" she yells.

My gut twists. "Gia, I really don't. You were fine earlier. Did I say something?"

"You act like everything's fine. Like you're fine. But you're not."

The words land like a slap. I'm halfway through forming a reply when the door cracks open and her hand shoots out. She shoves her phone into mine and slams the door again.

I look down.

Photo memory. *Looking Back – 2023.* It's the three of them—my parents, Gia in the middle, squished in tight. All smiles. Her cello recital. This exact day last year.

"Oh, fuck," I whisper. I knew it was coming up, but I blocked it out so well I didn't realize the day had arrived.

"Gia," I say, pressing my forehead to her door. "I'm so sorry. I didn't realize... I didn't mean to ignore it. I've just been trying to keep moving."

"Go away," she says, barely audible.

So I do.

I carry her phone back to the kitchen and set it next to mine. The picture still glows. Her little grin, their faces pressed together. My chest tightens and I sniff away a tickle in my nose.

We inherited billions that night.

But I'd trade it all to sit with my dad and listen to his long-winded political theories. Or hug Mom and smell that stupid gardenia lotion she always wore. Money doesn't mean shit.

I swipe a tear from my cheek and grab my phone.

Hey. I know you haven't gotten back to me about us, but Gia's breaking down and I really need help. It's urgent. Please text or call me back.

I start the kettle. I don't even want tea, but I need something to do with my hands.

Before the water boils, my phone chimes.

I'm out at Healing Spirit.

Bring Gia over.

There's a dropped pin. East side of town. Back roads and horse trails.

I exhale.

It's time to go talk my little sister into getting out of bed. Time to stop trying to fix everything myself.

Twenty-Two

The Girlfriend

~~~

Beth

My body fidgets as I sweep Cocoa's stall. Any minute now, Will is going to show up—with his girlfriend—and ask me to fix her. Emotional emergency, he said. My help, he said.

Part of me wants to be professional, to show up and give her the space she needs. It's not her fault, after all.

The other part wants to call him out. Loudly. Because seriously, who brings their girlfriend to the therapist he just happened to sleep with?

I slam the broom down harder than necessary and yank the hose to fill Cocoa's trough.

"Aren't you in a state."

I jump. Jan's leaning against the barn wall, arms crossed, unreadable but knowing.

"Oh boy, am I," I huff.

"You wanna talk about it?" she offers, turning the spigot for me.

I take a breath. "Remember the guy I told you about? Will?"

She nods.

"Well, he just called and then texted. Apparently, he's having an emergency—with his *girlfriend*. And he wants *my* help."

"Big surprise," Jan mutters.

"I told him to bring her out here," I add, not quite meeting her eyes.

"You did what now?" Her laugh is rich and gravelly.

"Yeah, I know. I panicked. I figured, the sooner I rip this Band-Aid off, the better. If anything, it'll help me get over him."

Jan raises an eyebrow. "You plan on telling her about-?" She cuts off but moves her finger between me and the empty air. I get it. Will and I.

"No. It's not her fault he's an asshole. Why punish her for his mess?" I exhale. "Maybe she just needs someone in her corner."

Jan narrows her eyes. "Careful, Beth. You've got a good heart, but don't mix your personal life with your professional one. Boundaries, remember?"

Before I can answer, I hear the crunch of gravel. I wipe my hands on my jeans and brace myself.

Will climbs out of the truck, wearing dusty jeans, a worn t-shirt, and a ball cap. My stomach flips, unhelpfully.

And then the passenger door opens.

Not stilettos. Not long legs and model hair.

Climbing from the passenger seat is a young girl. A kid, really—messy ponytail, tear streaks through the dust on her cheeks, arms folded protectively across her chest.

I blink.

Will walks toward me. "Thanks for meeting us."

I nod, working hard to keep my expression neutral. "Of course."

"And who's this?" I ask gently.

Will's eyes soften. "Gia, this is Beth—the woman I told you about. Beth, this is my little sister."

Little sister. The realization crashes into me, and it must show because Will winces slightly. I recover quickly.

"Nice to meet you, Gia." I offer my hand.

She shakes it half-heartedly and stares at the ground. Still, she follows me and Will into the office. I keep the tone light, offering tea, lemonade, coffee, even cocoa. Gia picks tea. Will asks for coffee—two creams, one sugar.

Of course he does.

I bring the drinks back to find Gia inspecting a photo of a woman riding at sunset. Her eyes are softer now, curious.

"So, Gia," I say, easing into it, "what brings you here today?"

"I..." Her mouth opens, but the words catch. She looks down, fists clenching.

"It's okay," I offer. "You don't have to say anything until you're ready."

She starts to shake her head—then it all rushes out.

"It's not fair! They're gone! They're really gone, and they're not coming back, and it sucks and I miss them!"

I lower my voice. "Who, sweetheart?"

"My mom and dad!" she cries.

My throat clenches.

I glance at him. He's folded forward, elbows on knees, face hidden beneath the bill of his cap.

"It was a year ago today," he says quietly. "In an accident."

"I'm so sorry," I say softly. "That kind of loss... it's enormous."

"They're dead, and I can't even go visit their graves. And all we're doing is fixing a stupid fence!" Gia glares at Will, but it's pain, not anger, in her eyes.

"Is that what was wrong?" he asks, reaching to put an arm around her. She allows it—barely.

"Why didn't we fly home to see them?" she whispers.

"I guess..." Will's voice breaks. "I guess I didn't want to face it. I was trying to block it out. I thought... I thought you were handling it like I was."

"You mean not handling it?"

That lands.

"I didn't want to think about it," Will admits. "I knew the date was coming, so I just kept busy. I didn't realize how much you were hurting."

"Yeah, well *I am*! I think about it every day!" She shrugs him off and turns away.

I let the moment breathe. Sometimes the best thing a therapist—or a friend—can do is step back.

"Gia," I say gently, "how do you feel about going for a walk?"

She shrugs again.

"Do you like horses?"

Her posture straightens. "Yeah… I guess."

"Then let's go for a walk. Not as therapist and client, just as friends."

She looks at me, really looks at me, then nods.

We head outside, Will trailing behind. At the edge of the horse stalls, Gia stops and turns.

"Not you," she tells him. "I want to talk to her. Alone."

Will's jaw tightens, but he nods. "Okay."

"You sure?" I ask.

"I trust you," he says.

His words do something to my chest.

Just then Jan calls out from one of the stalls. "Hey, cowboy. I could use a hand."

Will turns to her, grateful for a distraction. I turn to Gia.

"You ready?"

She nods.

We walk together down a sandy trail behind the barn, past low brush and fading sunlight.

"You know," she says eventually, "he's trying really hard. He just sucks at showing it."

"That's fair," I say. "Sometimes when people don't know what to do with pain, they pretend it's not there."

I feel my inner impressions about Will begin to shift. I am not sure what to make of it, yet, but now's not the time to think about it. I focus on Gia's next words.

"I don't want to pretend. I want to remember."

"Then that's exactly what you should do. And maybe he should too, in his own time. For now, pretending might be the best he can do."

"Well it sucks." She kicks a bit of plant debris off the trail.

We talk. We don't talk. She tells me about her cello recital. About how they took her to dinner. About how she dreamed of her mom last week and woke up crying. I listen. Just listen.

When we come back around, the horses flick their ears as we pass. Gia slows down, then places a delicate touch on my arm.

"Can I meet them now?"

"Absolutely."

We spend twenty minutes at the stalls. She feeds them treats, asking each of their names. She even laughs when one snorts in her hair.

And then Will appears, standing at the fence, watching us.

Gia sees him, too. She doesn't roll her eyes or cross her arms.

She smiles.

"Can we go up to the lake sometime?" she asks.

"If we get our work done, sure," he says.

"I suggest Thursday," I chime in. "It's less crowded. But it's still spring so just a heads up, the water'll freeze your balls off."

Gia bursts out laughing.

Will smiles at her, then at me.

"Thanks," he says.

It takes me a moment to realize he means for the talk, not the vulgarity.

"She did the work," I tell him. Then, because I want to—because it feels right—I add, "I gave her my number. Just in case she ever needs to talk."

His eyes soften.

"And I meant it when I said I'm not your therapist," I say to Gia, "but if you ever need someone to talk to… I'm here." I look at Will and add, "And you, too."

I can't believe I say it. But I do.

He doesn't reply right away. Just gives me a long, quiet look. Then nods.

"Thank you."

And for the first time in a long while, I don't feel like I'm standing across enemy lines. I feel like we might be on the same side. I won't say he's boyfriend material, but maybe he's not so bad.

Twenty-Three

Hello, Butterflies

Beth

"Can you bring your dad his lunch?" Mom had asked.

"Sure," I'd said.

What was I thinking?

Dad isn't normally absent-minded—forgetting Missy's world-class pastrami with pickles and Dijon mustard is unheard of. Yet when she found it sitting abandoned on the bench by the door, she'd summoned me to drive it to him 'without delay.'

Of course, that means heading out to Will's ranch, but that shouldn't be a problem. A few days have passed since they visited Healing Spirit—plenty of time to get my head right where he's concerned. My heart's settled now. Will's good-looking, charming, and firmly "look, don't touch." Besides, Gia has texted a few times, and honestly, I'm looking forward to seeing how she's doing.

My stomach betrays my resolve, twisting uncomfortably as I navigate toward the Fitzgerald Ranch, trying—and failing—to ignore the fluttering anticipation.

The property unfolds ahead, expansive and sun-baked, bathed in fierce

Sunrises and Sagebrush

Nevada sunlight. Dust billows into my open window as I park beside a neat stack of lumber. Near the fence, my dad stands in his element, sleeves rolled up, gesturing broadly at Will and Gia. Will looks mildly perplexed but nods politely, while Gia holds a hammer between her hands like it's a prize, hanging on every word my dad says.

Looks like he's found himself a Padawan, I laugh to myself.

Dad spots me first and raises a weathered hand, grinning widely. "Hot damn! You saved me!" He claps Will on the shoulder and adds, "No matter how many posts we get up, the day would've been a wash without my pickle 'n pastrami."

"I'd hate to see that day," I tease, holding up the insulated bag. "Mom made extras, so there's enough for everyone."

Will's eyes meet mine briefly, something sparkling behind them before he turns back to my dad. Gia balances her hammer carefully on the wooden post before sprinting toward me, eyes alight.

"Sick!" she gushes enthusiastically. "I'm starving to death!"

She reaches eagerly for the bag, fingers already tugging at the canvas until I tilt it toward her. Together, we peel it open like kids at Christmas.

Will gives her an exaggerated scowl. "Hey, watch it, piranha. Beth needs her fingers."

"Nahhh!" I wave off his comment playfully. "It's the joy of being a psychologist—I don't need my fingers to talk."

Dad ambles up beside us, peering over Gia's shoulder with mock impatience. "Well, if I don't get my sandwich soon, I might have to eat 'em myself."

"They're hot!" Gia exclaims excitedly, pulling a foil-wrapped sandwich from the bag.

"Oh, she didn't!" Dad glances sideways at me, pure glee lighting his face.

"She definitely did," I confirm with a wink, returning to the open driver's door. Mom couldn't just make extra sandwiches; she grilled them all until the meat was warm and cheese oozed deliciously from the edges. "And…" I reach inside and lift out a sealed pitcher that sloshes gently with iced tea and ice cubes. "She made orange sunrise tea, and I nabbed some chips and apples on my way out."

"Wow," Will murmurs appreciatively, examining the sandwich as I grab the remaining food and hip-check the door closed. "I thought it was us who were supposed to make you lunch," he says, teasing my dad lightly.

"I'll invoice you," Dad retorts as he snatches his own foil brick, grinning.

Gia giggles, confidently taking a giant bite, melted cheese dripping onto her fingers. She rolled her eyes in exaggerated delight. "Oh my God," she mumbles into her sandwich, "so good!"

I set everything out on the truck bed, and Gia hops up, making herself comfortable against the cab. Dad and Will lean casually against the truck near me, quietly relishing their first bites of hot pastrami.

"I didn't expect you today," Will says eventually, his voice soft and careful.

I hand him a cup filled with cold, sweet hibiscus-orange tea. "Missy's sandwiches are legendary," I reply lightly, keeping my tone casual. "And I figure you might appreciate something edible after what I assume has been several hours of... fence-related TED Talks."

Will laughs quietly, glancing toward my dad. "You have no idea. I've learned more about screws in the last hour than I learned about my job in fifteen years."

"Well, not all screws are created equal," I smile, glancing over at my dad, who shakes his head, chuckling. "You put a drywall screw into a horse fence, it'll go flying the second the wind blows."

Will laughs harder now. "He literally said exactly that earlier."

"Huh." I shrug innocently. "What're the odds?"

"He's a good man," Will says warmly, giving me a sidelong glance. "Easy to see where you get your intelligence... and sarcastic wit."

"Hey," I feign offense, "I prefer 'refined sense of humor.'"

"Fair enough," Will concedes easily.

But Dad isn't buying it. "Honey, I don't think they call it refined. The word you're looking for is 'uncouth.'" He takes a long swig of tea.

"Lewd," I add, biting into my apple with a rude crunch.

"Coarse!" Gia chimes in from the truck bed.

"Nailed it!" I say, tossing her a bag of chips.

Will covers his mouth with a fist, shoulders shaking silently with laughter.

A comfortable silence settles as Gia enthusiastically demolishes her chips. Despite occasional nerves when my eyes meet Will's, I'm doing fine. I think I got this.

After we finish, Gia eagerly offers to show me their progress, but Dad glances meaningfully between Will and me, gesturing Gia back. It's like the old man knows something I don't.

As we tour the ranch, Will leads me around, showing off their hard work. The stable gleams with freshly sealed wood, and a nearly-complete fence stretches proudly around it. An immaculate four-rail paddock gate leans against the stable, ready for installation.

"This is incredible," I say sincerely. "You've done so much in just a couple weeks."

Will's expression is proud and a bit distant. "We had a little help with the stall, but Gia's been up early every morning, keeping me on my toes."

"You picked out a horse yet?" I muse aloud, admiring the stall thoughtfully placed against the afternoon sun, perfect for shelter.

"Not yet. We're waiting until it's fully finished, so Gia doesn't get attached to a horse that might sell before we're ready." His smile dims slightly. "Listen, Beth, about the other night—"

My heart stutters briefly, but I keep my expression calm. "It's okay, Will. Really."

"No, it's not. It didn't come out right." He rubs his thumb nervously over a spot on his jeans. "I shouldn't have left so quickly. Gia and I... we've been carrying a lot."

"Of course you have," I reply gently. "Grief complicates everything."

He meets my eyes, sincere and searching. "I just don't want you thinking badly of me."

Hello, butterflies.

"I don't," I assure him quietly. "We're all healing. Sometimes it's messy."

He exhales slowly, visibly relieved. "You're pretty insightful, you know that?"

"Oh, I'm aware." I inject teasing confidence that draws out his reluctant smile.

He watches Gia animatedly gesturing at my dad, then says quietly, "We're heading back to Texas next week—to visit their graves. My aunt can be difficult… Her opinions and expectations can be…" he trails off, searching.

"Hard," I finish softly. "Family expectations usually are."

He nods, tension easing slightly from his shoulders. "Exactly. And we still have a lot to finish here if we want to open this year."

"A week or two won't hurt," I reassure him. "My dad can keep a crew going in his sleep. You'll barely recognize the place when you get back."

Will laughs warmly. "I have no doubt."

"If it means anything," I add gently, "I think you're doing right by her."

He looks surprised but deeply pleased. "Coming from you, that means a lot."

"Beth!" Gia calls excitedly. "You have to see my sketch! Ben said it's genius!"

Dad chuckles. "I said ambitious, but sure, genius works."

Will smiles fondly. "Better go—Miss Genius awaits."

When I reach her, Gia proudly thrusts her sketchbook into my hands, eyes bright and hopeful. "Wow, Gia," I breathe, genuinely impressed. "This is seriously amazing."

"You really think so?" Her voice softens with vulnerability. "I know Will worries, but…I just feel it, you know?"

I nod warmly. "Your dreams should scare you a little. That's how you know they're big enough."

She beams with relief. "See? Beth gets me!"

Will, watching silently, gives me an approving nod.

My chest tightens, warmth blooming inside me. "I was a girl with big dreams once too."

I shrug one shoulder, trying not to indicate the impact the moment is having on me.

"Alright," Dad claps his hands together and clomping toward the fence. "Back to work. This fence won't build itself."

"Thank goodness we've got an expert," Will says sincerely, moving to follow Dad back to the posts.

"Hey," I blurt before the idea is fully hatched in my mind, "How do you feel about going riding with me tomorrow morning? If it's okay with Will of course." I glance quickly his way but keep my attention fixed on Gia.

"That'd be fire!" Gia beamed ear to ear.

"Are you sure you wouldn't mind?" Will raises an eyebrow.

"Mind? I could seriously use the girl time. Carol is alright but a little too gruff for a casual morning jaunt." I smile at Gia and as enthusiastic as that young woman already is, I swear she brightens.

We say our goodbyes. I cross paths with Will as he goes for the fence and I for the driveway.

He pauses briefly near me, his voice low, "Thanks for today."

"Of course," I reply, my heart light and heavy all at once. "That's what friends are for."

His eyes search mine, catching the boundary I gently place between us. He nods once, respectful, understanding. "Friends," he repeats with confidence, and then walks back to join Gia and my dad.

I watch them for a moment longer, the sun warm on my shoulders, uncertainty tangled with something sweeter. So we can be friends. Honestly, that's exactly what I need and more than I hoped for.

Twenty-Four

Talk About a Dom

Beth

The morning air is fresh, sharp with the scent of sagebrush and wet dirt from last night's rain. A brisk but gentle breeze blows as Gia and I lead Gypsy and Dancer along the fenced pen behind my parents' house. Gia strokes Dancer's neck with gentle, confident hands, murmuring quiet nonsense to calm the mare. I watch, smiling to myself. For all her youthful bravado, Gia has a real knack with animals.

"You sure you're ready?" I ask as we pause by the mounting block. "It's okay to take your time."

Gia scoffs playfully, rolling her eyes. "C'mon, Beth, I got this. Grandpa put me in a saddle before I could walk." She pauses thoughtfully, correcting herself. "Well, maybe not literally. But basically."

I chuckle softly. "Alright, cowgirl, have at it."

Gia steps onto the mounting block and swings herself easily into Dancer's saddle, adjusting her posture with a moment's unsteadiness as she settles into place. Within a minute, I see her posture straightening. I release a held breath. Still a tad wary of her riding skills, I climb onto Gypsy, sensing the mare's shifting movement beneath me.

"Alright, Gyps," I murmur, patting her neck. "You're a beautiful girl, aren't you?"

We start with wide, easy circles around the enclosed pen, and Gia quickly finds her rhythm. She guides Dancer with a gentle, assured hand, clearly comfortable despite the years away from riding.

"Looking good, Gia," I call encouragingly.

"Yeah?" Her grin is broad and proud and she turns toward me with confidence. "Told ya I still had it!"

After a few minutes, she gestures toward me with excitement. "Hey, you think I could try Gypsy?"

I hesitate briefly, considering. "Gypsy's a little tricky. She doesn't warm up to people easily."

"Totally get that," Gia says, not at all deterred. "I swear, horses are way easier than people. You just gotta talk their language."

I laugh despite myself, loving her confidence. "Okay, you convinced me. But if she acts up, don't push it. And I'll be watching closely. Deal?"

"Deal," Gia nods firmly.

We dismount and swap horses, Gia approaching Gypsy slowly and confidently. She offers her hand for Gypsy to sniff, murmuring softly. "Easy, Gyps, we're gonna be friends, I promise."

Gypsy's ears flick uncertainly, but she allows Gia to mount without fuss. My chest tightens with hopeful surprise as Gia begins walking her slowly around the pen. Gypsy's muscles relax beneath Gia's soft guidance, her typically wary expression softening.

"Wow," I whisper, genuinely impressed. "She likes you! That's rare."

Gia grins over her shoulder, practically glowing. "Told ya! You just gotta speak horse."

After several calm laps, we move out onto the open trail. Side by side, we ride in comfortable silence, the rhythm of the horses' steps soothing beneath us.

Eventually, Gia shoots me a glance. "Hey, I signed up to help out at this community pantry downtown—first and third Saturdays. I figured it's something I can do besides just ranch work."

I smile at her. "That's really cool. People don't expect young teens to take initiative on much, but you've got it in droves."

She shrugs, trying to play it casual, but I catch the flicker of pride in her expression. "We just get underestimated is all."

"You'll meet a lot of great people through something like that," I add. "Just don't forget to find some time for people your own age too."

She tilts her head. "You mean like friends-friends?"

"Yeah. People you can be your whole teenage self around. You deserve that."

"I've got a few online. From Newport. We still talk on Discord. And there's this girl I met at school named Megan. She's kind of awesome."

I raise an eyebrow. "Kind of awesome?"

Gia grins. "Fine, she's very awesome. She's into hiking and true crime, and we both think root beer is the best soda and play FNAF."

"Finaff?" I question.

Gia rolls her eyes. "Five Nights at Freddie's. It's a horror game. Kinda. It's about these animatronics in a pizza parlor that eat people! You know, jump scares and stuff. It's so much fun!"

"Ah, a real bond."

She snorts. "Exactly."

We ride quietly for a few more minutes before she gives me a mischievous look. "So… speaking of making friends, let's talk about you." She draws out the 'you' conspiratorially.

"Oh boy," I say, rolling my eyes. "Is this about Will?"

"Duh," Gia says bluntly. "He's crushing on you, like big-time."

I raise a skeptical eyebrow. "Ph, I doubt that. He's just charming to everyone."

I don't tell her that just the comment makes my heart swell and my head spin.

She huffs dramatically. "Are you kidding? He's practically heart-eyed every time you show up. It's kinda gross, actually." She fakes a gag, even using her shoulders for effect.

I laugh softly, shaking my head. "Gia, trust me. Will and I are the last people who should be thinking about relationships right now. He's still healing, and honestly, I'm coming off something pretty yucky myself."

Gia sighs dramatically. "Ugh, fine. Crush my dreams."

I smile softly, nudging Dancer closer to her. "Your dreams, huh?"

"Yeah, you're nice and fun and you talk to me like I'm a real person. The last chick he brought home talked to me like I was five."

"Oh, no! How old were you?" I am not fishing for how long it's been since he took someone home at all.

"I don't know, maybe five or so." She hears her own words and adds, "but that doesn't mean she needed to talk to me like one."

I can't help laughing. "Well, not to dash your dreams but neither of us needs more complications right now."

"Whatever," she grumbles, then perks up brightly. "You guys are still shipped."

"You shipped us?" I tease gently.

"Yeah! You know, OTP, heart-eyes-forever, total endgame." She nods like a sage.

I chuckle. "Okay, noted."

She gives me a hopeful look. "But like, we're still gonna hang out, right? 'Cause I'm totally claiming you as my friend, even if Will's not boyfriend material."

"Absolutely," I reassure her. "Friendship is non-negotiable."

Her smile returns, satisfied, and we ride on in peaceful silence, letting the horses find a steady rhythm beneath us.

After a while, Gia breaks the quiet again. "Hey, Beth? Can I ask you something?"

"Shoot," I reply.

She takes a breath, focusing ahead. "So, this whole going-back-to-Texas thing—visiting my parents' graves—it just feels… weird, you know? Like, what am I even supposed to do there?"

I glance sideways, touched by the vulnerability in her voice. "Honestly? Just be there. Feel whatever comes up. That's enough."

"Yeah, I guess." She frowns thoughtfully, then adds, "It's not just the graves, though. My Aunt Cathy—she's… a lot."

"A lot?" I prompt.

Gia leans in, whispering conspiratorially. "She's like a total Dom."

I nearly choke on laughter. "Gia, do you even know what that means?"

She waves me off. "Yeah, obviously. It means she's in charge and bosses everyone around."

I bite back another laugh and nod. "Close enough."

Gia giggles proudly. "She always acts like she knows what's best—especially for Will. She tries to control everything, and he totally hates it. But he won't say anything 'cause she's family."

"That sounds tough," I say gently. "Maybe he's afraid of disappointing her."

Gia nods, her voice quiet. "Exactly. That's why this ranch thing is so huge, Beth. It's not just about me. It's about Will finally doing his own thing. Finally proving Aunt Cathy wrong."

"You're pretty insightful, you know that?" I say.

She blushes, feigning modesty. "Sure do."

We continue down the trail quietly, but Gia's innocent teasing about Will lingers stubbornly in my mind. Her words continue to send ripples through me, making it hard to focus on the moment. Despite myself, the idea takes root. Maybe, just maybe, Gia's right, and there's something more to this—something worth considering, once we've both had time to heal.

Right now the only thing I need to focus on is the warming air, the trail ahead, and the company of a young woman who reminds me a lot of a younger version of myself.

Twenty-Five

Slow Burn Manipulation

Will

The air is hot and muggy, soaked in silence. It's a different kind of heat from the desert. It's oppressive; it sticks to your skin. There isn't a bird or a breeze, not a breath out of place. Only the echo of our footsteps as Gia and I walk the gravel path through the Fitzgerald family plot.

Already, I miss Nevada. The revelation surprises me. The air back home is drier, cleaner. Somehow lighter. Even the quiet is different. Out there, stillness feels like space to breathe. Here, it presses in like a weight.

We stop at the entrance gate—wrought iron painted black, flanked by tall stone markers etched with a few family names I barely remember and many I don't know at all. The Fitzgeralds are nothing if not thorough with legacy. Our parents are buried in the far corner, beneath a pair of sleek granite headstones that match nothing else in the plot. Mom's choice. She'd picked them long before the accident, not knowing they'd be planted here instead of California.

Gia walks a half-step behind me, her grip tight on the bouquet of lilies in her hands. She hasn't said much since we landed. I haven't pushed.

The path crunches beneath us as we near the graves. My chest tightens.

The markers are too clean, too new, too sharp against the soft greenery that clings to the others around them. Out of place. Just like they were.

"Feels weird, doesn't it?" Gia's voice is quiet, her gaze fixed forward.

"Yeah," I say. "They never belonged here."

She kneels and places the flowers carefully in front of our mom's headstone. Her fingers brush the engraved name with a gentleness that guts me.

"I thought I'd cry," she says after a long silence. "Like... ugly cry. But I don't feel anything."

I don't know what to say, but Beth's words echo in my mind. "Remember what Beth said? It's okay to feel whatever you feel."

"I feel like I'm an awful daughter." She lets out a heavy sigh.

"No," I sink to a crouch beside her. "You're not awful."

She sniffs once, wipes her nose. "I thought I'd feel something big. Like lightning. Closure or peace or... I don't know. But it's just—nothing. Like I'm watching it happen to someone else."

I nod. I feel it too. That strange numbness, like we're standing in a photograph instead of real life. I know their bodies are right here before us but part of me refuses to believe it, even after a year. I wish Beth were here to tell me what to say.

"I think sometimes grief- well, it hides. Deep down." I say, stumbling awkwardly through it. "It waits for the right moment. Sometimes it doesn't show up until you're making pancakes or cleaning the barn and suddenly—bam."

She lets out a shaky laugh. "That's specific." Then she puts her arm around me. She gets it.

We sit in silence. A breeze stirs the tall grass near the fence line. Gia reaches for my hand and links our fingers. It reminds me of when she was three or four and I used to keep her hand linked with mine so she wouldn't run off. Now she is using the connection to remain grounded in an entirely different way. I feel a painful tightening in my chest.

"I hate it here," she says finally. "This place. These people. I miss grandpa. Texas isn't home without him. Mom and Dad agree, you know."

I do know. I imagine their spirits out there, uneasy, wishing they were resting comfortably back home.

"I think they would have liked Nevada."

Gia's observation hits me out of the blue and as I turn to her, my eyes well up with tears. I fight the urge to wipe them away. *Just feel whatever it is you feel.*

Gia sees my tears and they catch, causing her giant, warm brown eyes to well up with moisture of their own. The dam finally breaks. We cry on and off—sometimes together, sometimes alone. We tell stories about our parents or dream up what they would do on the ranch back in Nevada. We laugh between tears and cry between laughing. It hurts. But it feels good.

After a while, we are both on empty. We sit in silence for a while, just staring at the ground or up at the sky.

Gia wipes her face with her sleeve and snorts. "I probably look like I got punched in the face." She lets out an ironic giggle.

"Just tell them 'you should see the other guy,'" I suggest.

"You're a dork." She elbows me.

"I know," I say.

I glance over at her. "You wanna head out?"

She pauses, then shakes her head. "No. Why couldn't we just get a hotel while we are here? Why do we have to stay at the," her voice drips with disgust, "Fitzgerald Legacy Ranch?"

I twinged at her tone, thinking of the name I'd put on the deed for our own little ranch estate.

I answered coolly, "I don't want to be there any more than you do, but Cathy texted me earlier. Something about paperwork for grandpa's estate."

Of course. Always something with Cathy. It couldn't be an emotionally cleansing few days to honor our parents. It has to be all about her.

"She'll probably have you shredding ten years worth of her own business garbage."

Ah! Gia remembered the last time we visited the ranch, a few months after grandpa's death. Cleaning stalls was one thing. It built character. Doing her tedious office work was another.

"Yeah," I sigh. "Alright. Let's get it over with."

"Will, you're not seriously going to be her slave are you?" Gia put her hands on her hips.

"No, no. If it's anything like that, we will be on the next plane home. I promise."

We stand. I look back once at the headstones—those polished slabs that somehow look like strangers.

Mom. Dad. I love you and I hope we're doing you proud.

A Texas-style Garden Party

The Fitzgerald estate looks like it was plucked straight off a postcard titled *"The Old Money South"*—three stories of white stucco, black iron railings, and just enough ivy to whisper *we've been here longer than God*. It sits on a rise like it's judging the horizon.

Out back, the party is already underway. Relatives and friends from every dusty corner of the family tree mill around the veranda, sipping sweet tea and laughing in a restrained, upper-class way I hadn't noticed until now. *Pretentious*. Looks like Nevada is rubbing off on me. We pass Aunt Lorna near the dessert table—she gives us a charming smile and a princess wave but doesn't stop talking to a manicured man I imagine is her "tennis partner." Michael, my cousin and a carbon copy of his dad, nods at me from across the patio, phone already in hand like he's timing how long we stay.

The breeze carries the scent of roses and hairspray—a combination seared into memory and instantly stomach-turning. Aunt Cathy's nearby.

Gia and I barely get two steps through the door before we're ambushed by kisses, voluptuously chested hugs, and southern squeals.

"Lord above! There's my sweet babies!" Aunt Cathy coos in fluent Southern Baptist. "Oh, my word—Will, don't you just look exactly like your daddy. And Gia, honey, you've grown into such a lady."

She's in a pale pink pantsuit, the kind with shoulder pads sharp enough to signal planes. Her hair is a cloud of curls that defies both age and gravity. The shade of blonde against her weathered skin isn't fooling anyone.

I breathe in shallowly as the smell that alerted me to her presence threatens to overtake me. I flash the smile I save for sales pitches and pyramid schemes. "Aunt Cathy! Looking radiant as ever."

"Oh!" She blushes and looks sideways at me, waving off the compliment in mock humility. "Aren't you just the sweetest thing!"

I pivot the conversation with practiced charm. "Nice turnout."

"Oh, sugar, it's just a little something I threw together. The Lord gives us reasons to gather, and I do so love when family comes home." She pats my cheek, then cups Gia's face like she's inspecting fruit at a farmer's market.

I glance around at faces I barely recognize—and more than a few I've never seen. Not one of them looks like they make less than an eight-figure income. I doubt she just *threw this party together*, and I doubt it's in honor of anyone other than Aunt Cathy herself.

"I've missed you both so much," she continues. "But I'm getting ahead of myself. You two must be exhausted. That flight from Nevada is no joke."

"It's fine," Gia says, managing not to flinch. "We're glad to be here."

Cathy links her arm through mine like she's leading me to the altar. "Now don't wander off—I've had Gregory set up some paperwork inside for you to peek at later. Just a few little items from the estate. Nothing urgent, but we do like to keep things tidy."

Ah. There it is. And in under five minutes. A new record.

"Appreciate that," I say smoothly. "But we were hoping to just settle in for the day. Maybe catch up with some folks first?"

"Oh, of course! We wouldn't dream of dragging you into business straight away." She clutches her pearl necklace like someone just cursed. "This is a celebration of life. And family. But when you're ready, there are a few... legacy items that need your thoughtful touch. The Fitzgerald name does carry certain expectations, after all."

I nod, sipping my sweet tea like it might turn into whiskey if I wish hard enough. "It sure does." I force myself to smile. I remember Beth's tea—lightly sweetened and subtly flavored. What I'm holding now is more sugar than tea. For a second, I actually miss the desert.

Gia steps in, no chessboard in hand. "But our parents' estate is already settled, right?"

She hasn't had the years of careful conversational fencing. She's used to being tousled and spoiled and told how big she's getting. She's never had to sit in on family discussions or keep up with email chains.

Cathy's smile doesn't even wobble. "Of course, of course. Your dear daddy was thorough in his own way. But Grandpa's estate is a bit more… communal. As executor, it's my humble duty to ensure his legacy remains unified."

Translation: If we don't fall in line, we don't get a dime.

"But no pressure," she adds, practically singing. "You'll make the right choices. I've always believed in you, Will. And your little project out West? It's very… ambitious."

"Appreciate the vote of confidence," I say, smiling through my molars. "We're excited about it."

"Well, praise be!" she exclaims, patting my arm with a manicured hand that's probably signed more checks than I've ever seen. "But let's make sure we're building something that lasts. Not all dreams are… fiscally sound."

I feel Gia stiffen beside me but say nothing. There's nothing to say—not here.

"I'll look over whatever you've prepared," I reply. Then, I point across the lawn. "Is that Uncle Don?"

"It is!" she says brightly, then leans in, lowering her voice just enough to sound conspiratorial. "Did you hear what happened to him?" Not waiting for an answer, she continues. "His daughter up and married a boy from the city. He's an auto mechanic. Goes to community college." She shivers in disgust, then lowers her voice even further. "You know those places are breeding grounds for all sorts of bad ideas. No, I'm afraid the poor girl is lost."

Gia nudges me gently with her elbow, murmuring, "You need a parachute?"

I shake my head and give her a silent shush—but I smile and wink to let her know I appreciate the assist.

Aunt Cathy, oblivious, keeps her eyes on her 'disappointing' brother. When she turns back to us, her gaze sparkles with renewed faux warmth. "I'm so thankful you're nothing like her. I just know you two are going to make great choices."

She winks, then floats off to greet another guest like she didn't just threaten to cut us off with a sugar-dipped blade.

Once she's out of earshot, Gia mutters, "She's like a Disney villain with a Pinterest board."

I stifle a laugh. "Welcome home."

We drift toward the hors d'oeuvres, but the air's heavier now. There's a version of me that wants to walk out—leave the tea, the estate, the strings attached. But Gia's still beside me, and for her sake, I stay.

Looks like we're not just here for a weekend with our parents. We're here for strategy, signatures, and slow-burn manipulation disguised as garden parties. And I'm not sure which is worse—losing our inheritance or giving in to secure it.

Twenty-Six

You Remind Me of the Babe

Beth

The Fitzgeralds are out of town, and my life slides back into something like a normal rhythm. They've been gone about a week now, and while I've kept in light contact with Gia, everything feels quieter. Calmer. Like the dust has finally settled and I can see the shape of my life again.

Time has cooled whatever heat I felt for Will—along with the reminder that he's still grieving and trying to hold the pieces together. I don't blame him. I just know I can't wait around for someone else's healing to align with mine.

Spring has settled into the valley in full—warm mornings, moody thunderheads in the afternoons. Yellows, purples, and electric greens soften the gold-dust dirt and the scratchy sagebrush, flooding the desert with life. People think the desert's barren, but they couldn't be more wrong. You just have to look closer.

I fall into a routine: early jogs that don't kill me anymore, mornings with the horses and clients at Healing Spirit, online sessions Monday through Wednesday. It's the kind of work-hard, breathe-deep life I've craved since finishing my doctorate. Peaceful. Steady. It's only missing one thing:

Companionship.

The kind that won't ask me for more than I can give. The kind that doesn't expect answers I don't have yet.

Thursday afternoon rolls in slow and sunny, with no clients and my chores knocked out. I head down to the animal shelter to spend it meeting prospective best friends. I'm looking for a hiking buddy, someone to curl up with at night, a partner who can hang around the horses while I work. In other words: a dog.

I've got a mental checklist. Large breed. Not too young, not too old. Energetic but not unhinged. Good with livestock and kids. Maybe a retriever or a lab. Definitely not a puppy.

Which is why it's so inconvenient that the one who steals my heart is exactly everything—and absolutely nothing—on that list.

He's a ten-month-old Australian shepherd with a dark brown mask over crystal blue eyes and a coat like speckled silk—white, tan, and deep chocolate.

The second he's let out, he barrels toward me. I squat down just as he launches up, front paws on my chest, tongue already out like he's trying to lick his way into my soul.

"Well, aren't you forward?" I laugh, pressing my nose to his snout.

"That's Jerith!" chirps Paula, clipboard in hand and beaming. "Total cuddle bug. He just loves everybody. He's good with cats. Great with horses, too."

I groan inwardly. *Don't tell me that.*

Shepherds are smart. Trainable. Bred for livestock. Perfect. Except this dog is pure, unfiltered puppy.

He's only the fourth dog I've met today. There are two more waiting their turn, but I already know: there's no way I'm walking away from this one. Not after that hello. Not after those eyes.

"I think you can go ahead and start the paperwork," I say, scratching behind one speckled ear. "He's coming home with me."

Paula beams and leads me back to the office. Jerith trots beside me like we've been doing this forever.

"Did you say his name is *Jerith*?" I ask, arching a brow.

"Yep! We went with a *Labyrinth* theme for this litter. His sister was Sarah—

she got adopted this morning. I was sad they couldn't stay together. You haven't met Ambrosia yet—she's a Great Pyrenees, big ol' fluffball."

I grin. "Fitting," I say, picturing the movie. Then I glance down at Jerith. "But *you*... you don't look like a big, mean Goblin King, now do you?"

He cocks his head, then leaps up again, bumping against my leg mid-stride.

"No, you don't," I murmur, considering. "Hmm... fun, spunky, little mischief gremlin but uniquely handsome..."

It clicks. Just like that.

"How about *Bowie*?"

Paula claps. "I *love* it!" She crouches to scratch behind his ears. "Hello, Bowie."

Less than thirty minutes later, I'm driving home with the leash looped around my wrist and the windows cracked. Bowie's nose is smudging up the passenger window, ears flapping in the wind like he was born for this.

He fits. Already.

And I can picture Gia's reaction clear as day—squealing, grabbing his face, insisting he needs a matching bandana. She's going to lose her mind.

My chest tightens just a little. She's still stuck in Texas, dealing with sharks in pastel cardigans. I miss her. More than I thought I would.

But for now, I roll down the other window and let the wind rush through the cab. Bowie yips once—sharp and excited—then sticks his tongue out with the confidence of a creature who knows exactly where he belongs.

Just like that, Bowie Wilkes becomes the new man in my life.

Twenty-Seven

Gilded Guilt

―⁂―

Will

The library at the Fitzgerald estate is too warm, despite the vaulted ceilings and expensive air conditioning. I've shed my blazer, rolled up my sleeves, and popped the top button on my shirt, but the heat clings like a reminder—I'm not here for comfort.

It's been about ten days since we arrived in Texas, and most of that time has been spent in conference rooms, poring over paperwork with second cousins I barely know and dodging loaded questions from Aunt Cathy. Gia's been a good sport, ducking out for air when she needs it, while I've tried to shoulder most of the estate meetings myself. We signed what we had to, stalled what we couldn't, and politely danced around the rest. It's not done—but the dust has started to settle.

Aunt Cathy sits across from me at the long conference table, all Southern charm and sharpened edges. She's immaculate in a sleeveless silk blouse and heels that have never met a patch of grass. Her perfume is floral and commanding, like roses with a warning label. Her voice, sweet as sun tea, pours syrup over every word.

"I just *love* you two like you're my own," she says, reaching across the table like she might hold my hand in prayer. "I hated seeing your parents take you so far from us. It broke my heart, Will, truly it did. But I've always hoped you'd come back to the fold. Maybe now's the time."

Gregory, the estate lawyer, sits to her right, flipping through a folder thick enough to bruise someone. He's the human version of fine print. I nod along as Cathy continues.

"So, the question becomes," she says sweetly, her smile fixed and church-appropriate, "whether you want to remain a part of the family trust. Continue walking under the Lord's light, so to speak, and the Fitzgerald name will carry you far—with all the resources and blessings that come along with it."

Her tone is silk with sand underneath. Gregory glances at me, waiting for some sign that I'm playing ball.

"Or?" I ask.

"Or," Cathy echoes, as if tasting the idea for the first time, "you could take your little venture as far from the family legacy as your daddy did. I recall he cashed in a bit of his share to chase his ideas back East." She sighs, eyes going soft and sad. "Such a shame. He had potential. But he sure loved your mother and sentiment..." Heavy dramatic sigh, "Well, sentiment clouds judgment."

The smile never wavers. "Now, of course I'm not saying you don't have a claim. But with your parents gone, well—there's some ambiguity. I'd hate to dig through the weeds of it, but you know I will if I have to. Unless, of course, we're all on the same page."

She sips from her glass like we're just talking about weather, not war.

Anger bubbles low in my chest. That was a jab at my dad, a jab at our mother, and a threat—*all in one sentence*—with enough sugar to give a bishop a toothache.

"Now, I do *love* a good passion project," she continues, with the cheer of someone announcing a church bake sale. "Keeps the spirit young. But vacation rentals in the Nevada desert? That's more... personal indulgence than generational wealth. The Fitzgeralds aren't exactly in the business of boutique hobbies."

My phone buzzes in my lap. I glance down.

SUBJECT: Fitzgerald Ranch Estate — Final Estimate & Signed Build Contract

The irony hits me square in the gut.

That name—*Fitzgerald Ranch Estate*—felt powerful when I first typed it into the form. Like I was claiming something, honoring where we came from. But here, in this antique cathedral of money and manipulation, it just feels hollow. Like I've been branding something that was never mine to begin with.

I tap the screen to darken it.

Cathy notices. Of course she does.

"Problem, sweetheart?"

"Just work," I say lightly.

Gregory slides a new folder toward me. "These outline current holdings and projected distributions, contingent on participation in estate activities. Nothing's final, of course, but access depends on clarity of intent."

I flip through the pages, but it's all smoke and mirrors. Legal code dressed up in inheritance perfume.

"Take your time," Gregory offers.

"I will," I say. I close the folder gently. "I'll review it with Gia and our lawyer. We'll get back to you in thirty days."

Cathy smiles with all her teeth. "Of course, sugar. I'm sure you'll help Gia understand what's best. Just remember—dreams need a foundation to stand on. And the Fitzgeralds… we've been laying stone for generations."

I nod tightly. "This is quite a foundation."

A barbed hook, baited with everything I was raised to want. I tuck the folder under my arm and stand.

* * *

Gilded Guilt

Outside, the garden is thick with heat but easier to breathe. I find Gia under the old oak tree, legs crossed on a low stone bench, book in hand. She looks up when she sees me and smiles.

"Hey."

"Hey," I say. "Got something for you."

Her eyes light up as I pull out the tablet and hand it to her. "Is that…?"

"Build contract came through," I confirm. "Nevada. Cabins. All of it."

She scrolls through the email, beaming. "Will, this is amazing."

"Yeah. It is."

She looks at the folder under my arm. "But…?"

"But the money," I say. "The family trust. Cathy's playing the long game. She's threatening to withhold our shares if we don't fall in line."

Gia frowns, brow knitting. "Could she really?"

"She can't take it. Not legally. But she can delay, muddy it, turn it into a mess." I shrug. "I could sell our share outright. We'd walk away with a massive payout—but that's it. No more quarterly distributions. No safety net."

Gia stares at the ground for a beat, then lifts her head.

"The money's not worth it if the dreams become someone else's."

I study her, sharp and sincere. She's young, but she's not naïve. She knows what's at stake. And she still chooses the dream.

Maybe that's what I need, too. Maybe legacy isn't just what you inherit. Maybe it's what you *build*. I don't say any of that. But something in me shifts.

I hand her the tablet again. She taps through the final pages, and I see it in her face—that fierce determination, the kind that can turn blank land into a future.

"They're gonna be beautiful," she says softly. "The cabins."

I nod. And this time, I let myself smile. "Yeah. They are."

I sign on her behalf. The inheritance questions stay unanswered—for now. But we've made one thing clear: We're building something. And it's ours.

Gia leans into my shoulder, tablet still in her lap. "So what now?"

I glance down at the Fitzgerald folder. Heavy. Still unopened.

"Now," I say, letting my breath out through my lips, "we breathe."

She nods but her eyes linger on the tablet screen. Worry creeps back into her brow.

"Hey," I murmur, nudging her with my elbow. "Let's not worry about the eggs before we know they're spoiled."

She huffs a soft laugh. "That's not how the saying goes."

"It is now," I grin. "C'mon. I think it's time we got ourselves back home."

Twenty-Eight

Blue-Eyed Devil

Beth

"Wilkes?"

The voice pulls me from my thoughts. I've been watching bubbles rise and burst in my pint glass at the far end of Overland's bar, zoning out somewhere between my second beer and the half-eaten basket of beer-battered cheese curds in front of me.

I glance up to see a tall guy in a Carhartt jacket silhouetted near the entrance. For a moment, my heart stutters as my stupid brain thinks its Will, but the voice is all wrong, and this guy's at least a head taller. Plus, Will's still in Texas.

Relax, Beth.

A tall guy in a Carhartt jacket stands just inside the entrance of Overland, backlit by late sunlight. My brain does that weird half-jump, misfiring on something familiar, but it's not nerves—it's memory.

He walks closer, and I recognize him. Tall, lean, blue-eyed, familiar in a way I can't quite place.

I lift my glass. "Hey."

He slides onto the bar stool beside me, nodding toward Cassie behind the bar. "Hey Cass! I called in a to-go." He turns back, smiling. "Beth Wilkes. You remember me?"

I give a friendly shrug. "From Chuck's dinner, right?"

He huffs a laugh. "C'mon. We go way back. High school. Senior year track team?"

I stare for a second, then it clicks. "Wade Leavitt. *Leave-it* Leavitt. Damn—sorry. We were little assholes back then."

"Thanks for that," he says, mocking being wounded with his hand to his heart. "Years of therapy undone in one sentence."

He's not the skinny kid I remember. He's broader now and his muscles have gone from string beans to lean but powerful. And I didn't even remember those blue eyes.

"You filled out nicely," I say before I can catch myself.

"I finally ate enough Wheaties." He shrugs with a wink.

He turns to Cassie. "Hey, Cass. Slow night?"

"Slow as snail snot," she mutters, handing him a menu.

He orders a burger and Coke. She nods and taps it into the computer behind the bar.

Wade turns back to me. "I'm glad I ran into you. I meant to say hi at Chuck's thing, but you disappeared before I could."

"Yeah, that whole evening got a little chaotic."

He smiles like it doesn't bother him. "Well, I'm around. Been back in town a few years now. Working construction, some land consulting, trying to keep up with the locals."

He nods at my curds. "May I?"

I slide the basket between us. "Have at it."

We eat in companionable silence, the kind that doesn't feel awkward. He's easy to sit beside. That was true back in high school, too.

"You still running?" he asks after a moment.

"I recently got back into wogging."

"Wogging?" He turns and sets his elbow on the bar.

"Yeah, it's like jogging, but, you know, mostly walking." I shrug and he laughs. "You?"

He pats his stomach. "Not unless someone's chasing me. But seriously, how you been?"

I chuckle and lean back. "I've been good. Busy. Building a business."

"That the horse therapy thing I've heard about?"

"That's the one." I lift my glass in toast.

Small town. Of course he's already heard about it.

"Sounds legit," he says, and I can tell he means it. "You always had that... grit."

It's a simple statement, but it lands somewhere soft. I nod. "Thanks."

Cassie drops off his to-go bag and throws in an extra napkin with a wink. Wade pays, then hesitates.

"Hey... you free for dinner tomorrow? Just dinner," he holds up his fingers in a scouts promise, "I'm not tryina get something out of it, just catch up with an old friend."

I consider it. Not the implications—just the feeling. I don't feel pressure. I don't feel obligation. Just... maybe I'd like to see what else life has in store besides work and healing and surviving. And catching up with an old friend, well, acquaintance, sounds nice.

"Sure," I say. "Why not?"

We exchange numbers, and he heads out with a nod and a grin.

I settle back into my seat at the bar. Cassie disappears into the back, and I sit with the last sip of beer and the quiet hum of restaurant din.

There's a strange, satisfying steadiness to it all. A moment to myself amidst the chaos of a life upheaved. At first I felt utterly alone, but as the dust settles, the feeling is more like...whole.

I think about the conversation with Wade. No butterflies. No spiraling. And not a single thought about needing someone else to anchor me.

I swirl the last bit of beer and knock it back.

I've still got goals. Big ones. And I'm not waiting around for anyone else to validate them.

For the first time in a long while, I feel kind of... bulletproof. Besides, with Bowie's companionship, who could want for more?

Twenty-Nine

Homecoming

Will

Returning to Nevada isn't quite what I expect.

Even the drive from the airport feels different this time. The land is still stark and brown, a broad stretch of earth that refuses to soften for anyone—it's flanked on all sides by towering mountains, their foothills rising like walls, cradling the valley Gia and I now call 'Home.' Texas was open—green and sprawling and full of memory. But in this place I feel grounded, along with an undertone of anticipation.

Gia stretches out beside me, limbs splayed dramatically across the seat.

"Yes!" she yawns as we pull onto the gravel drive. "I am so ready to be home."

The word still catches me off guard. *Home*. I thought that was Newport Beach. I thought that was where we belonged. Yet it doesn't feel wrong.

I smile. "Yeah. It'll be good to settle in again."

"Settle?" she snorts, twisting to unbuckle. "I can't wait to move. I'm so tired of sitting and sitting and sitting." She gestures to summarize our entire travel day—the drive to the airport, the plane from Dallas-Fort Worth, the hour-long stretch south from Reno. It's been a marathon of patience neither of us had to begin with.

Still, she says home, and she means here. That's something.

She's already halfway to the porch by the time I kill the engine.

The front door swings open on silent hinges, letting out a soft breath of cool, citrus-scented air. The interior is clean, quiet. The grey flooring, the pale walls, the soft hum of the fridge—it's all so still. After ten days of tight-knit family gatherings, estate documents, and Cathy's carefully sharpened scripture, it's almost unnerving.

I step inside and pause. The house smells like lemon and linen and something warmer underneath—maybe sage. A candle flickers on the island beside a card that reads Welcome Home in elegant script. Chuck and Jane signed it.

Damn. They didn't just restock the fridge.

I drop my travel backpack on a bar stool and beeline for the fridge. It's full—meats, produce, eggs, milk, and, much to my delight, two kinds of beer. I grab a Battle Born, smirking at the branding. Chuck: 1, Will: 0.

Gia lets out a squeal of joy behind me. "Oh my gawd, look at all this food!"

"Yeah, they went all out," I say, tipping the bottle toward her lemonade in a makeshift toast.

"Beth too," she adds, raising her bottle.

Beth. I blink at the name. I haven't gone a day without thinking about her.

"What do you mean?" I ask, trying to keep my voice casual.

Gia holds up a small care package tied with a sagebrush-green ribbon. "It was on my bed."

A brown bear clutches a flat, green leather journal with a tree pattern pressed into the cover. A sleek pen is tucked into the strap. Gia holds a note to her chest, refusing to share.

"People always get me baby stuff," she says, inspecting the journal. "Unicorns. Glitter. Stuff they think girls are supposed to like. Beth gets me."

"She still got you a teddy bear," I point out.

"He's a brown bear, not some derpy teddy." She hugs him protectively. "He's a comfort bear. The note says he's microwavable."

"You're not putting that thing in the microwave."

She's already crossing the kitchen. "It's designed for it."

The microwave dings a few seconds later. She pulls out the bear and tosses it to me.

"Here. Feel this."

It's warm. Soft. Weighted. Faintly lavender-scented and strangely comforting.

"Nice," I admit, tossing it back. "Just don't melt it."

She disappears down the hallway with a happy hum, her bear in one arm, journal in the other.

I sigh and head out to grab our luggage before I talk myself out of it. Tonight, there will be no meal prep. No healthy intentions.

I'm ordering pizza.

* * *

It's dark by the time I drag myself toward my bedroom. I don't bother turning on the overhead light—just reach for the lamp near the bed.

That's when I see it.

Another package, nearly identical to Gia's, sits neatly at the foot of my bed. Deep brown journal. Green ribbon. But my comfort item?

A plush grilled cheese sandwich.

I stop and laugh. It's so absurd, so perfect, that I can't even pretend to be annoyed.

I sit down and pick it up, half-expecting it to smell like butter and shame. Instead, it's sage—earthy and warm. I remember the conversation clearly: coffee shop banter, me defending my childhood comfort food, her horrified reaction to the concept of mayo on white bread. She'd wrinkled her nose and called it "a war crime."

She'd remembered.

I turn the little plush over in my hands. It has stubby little hands and feet and a soft orange center where the "cheese" oozes out. It's ridiculous. And completely endearing.

I find the note tucked beneath the journal:

I hope these find you with a mended heart.

The journal is for writing letters to your parents.

The sandwich is to bring you comfort.

It's microwavable—but DON'T dip it in tomato soup.

30 sec intervals until it's snuggly and warm.

Wishing you peace in small things,

—Beth

I stare at the handwriting a moment longer than I mean to.

It's late and I'm tired. Yet my heart feels strangely soft in my chest. I place the note and the journal on the nightstand, then carry the sandwich to the kitchen and toss it into the microwave.

Why not?

Thirty

Chocolate Lasagna

~~~~~

Beth

To say dinner is pleasant would be an understatement. We meet at Cook'd, a local favorite of mine, and fall into easy conversation over tri-tip salad and rib eye, football banter, and the politics of Niners loyalty.

"Yeah, but I have more right than you," I say, raising an eyebrow. "I just moved back from the Bay."

"True," Wade concedes, "but I played for the Niners in Pop Warner, so... close second?"

He gives me a pair of puppy-dog eyes that I *almost* pretend to be immune to.

"Okay, fine. And for college ball you're solidly—?"

"Wolf Pack," we say at the same time.

"Phew," I swipe the back of my hand across my forehead in mock relief. "Thought I was gonna have to walk out before the entrees."

"Northern Nevada loyalty," he says, raising his glass.

I clink mine against his. We drink like two friends who've spent the last ten years bantering over beers. He's easy to talk to and we've already agreed it's not a date. I'm paying for my own food, and he swore an oath on his

Cub Scout honor not to test my boundaries. So pretenses are off the table, allowing me to relax into the conversation.

The drinks flow, the food arrives, and his Christopher Walken impression nearly makes me spit-take my water. It's terrible. And I love how committed he is to selling it.

"I got a fever," I say, gesturing with both hands. "And the only prescription... is more cowbell."

"Moah cowbell," he repeats, and it's still awful.

The waitress arrives just in time with our food, smiling politely as she sets the plates down.

We stop talking as we eat. The air between us grows quiet, but not awkward. There's a comfort to the silence, like I can finally exhale. For a while, I forget everything else.

Then Wade leans back in his chair, wipes his hands on a napkin, and says casually, "I meant to say hi at Chuck's party, but you were busy playing cornhole with that filthy opportunist."

My fork pauses mid-bite. My open mouth shifts into, "Huh?"

"You know. Fitzgerald." He shrugs as he rubs the last bite of his steak around in the juices left on the plate.

I blink, caught off guard by the turn. "Will?"

He leans over his plate. "How much do you actually know about him?"

I hesitate, trying to decide if I want to tell him. Eventually, I offer a guarded, "Not much. Why?"

He shrugs, sips his drink, and continues. "I'd been saving up for that ranch—the one he bought. Silver Sage. I was working construction, hustling to get the down payment. Had an informal agreement with the Mackenzies. It wasn't locked in, but we were close. Then boom—outbid. Full cash offer. Gone."

"That sucks," I say honestly. "I'd probably be pissed too."

"Yeah, well, that's not the part that really gets me." He leans back again, voice casual but firm. "That article everyone keeps talking about—the one about bringing life back to the valley?"

I nod. "I haven't read it, but people won't shut up about it."

"In it, he says the whole thing's for his sister. That he bought the ranch to honor her dream. Talks about building something meaningful for her, creating legacy, all that PR gold." He grabs another fry and gestures loosely. "So I looked up the deed."

My stomach tightens, just a little. "And?"

"Name on it? William Jonathan Fitzgerald." He pops the fry. "Not Gia."

I sit back slowly, beer forgotten. "Huh."

"Yeah. Just feels... off, you know?" He shrugs like it's no big deal, but the seed is planted. "Whole humble cowboy thing? I think it's a pitch. He's not local. Doesn't care about the land. Just another rich kid playing rancher."

Our server drops off my favorite dessert—a slab of chocolate lasagna—and Wade thanks him with a grin.

The moment passes as we move on to safer topics. But thoughts and feelings linger.

I pick at my dessert, smiling when Wade dives in with gusto, but I'm now officially somewhere else. I'd told myself the gifts I left—Beth-branded care packages with journals and comfort snugglies—were just kindness. That the thank-you text from Will wasn't anything more than polite acknowledgment. That Gia's photo with her bear squished against her cheek didn't mean I'd gotten attached.

But suddenly, I wonder if I did too much. Gave too easily.

Did I misread him? Why does it matter?

* * *

By the time dessert is half-finished, Wade leans around the edge of the table and kisses me.

It's sweet. Unexpected. Soft. And completely devoid of fire. I kiss him back out of instinct or habit maybe. I don't want to hurt his feelings. But inside, I already know the truth.

There's no zing. No current. No thunderbolt behind the ribs or even a flutter in the gut.

"Sorry," I say, smoothing my hair back. "I just...I'm not-"

He waves it off. "No, I'm sorry. I should've asked. You were just—*so* beautiful, snorting whipped cream out of your nose."

I laugh, and most of the awkwardness dissolves with the joke.

I consider that this is what healing looks like—no more hot-guy radar. No more leaping into attraction like its bait on a fishing line. Maybe I've finally built in some insulation. Then again, there's that thank-you text from Will—brief, oddly specific. I've reread it more than once.

Am I going to fact check Wade's accusations? You're damn right I am, but not because I want to get tangled up with either man. I just like to have the facts. What I do with them, well, that is for future me to figure out.

I shake my head and focus on the layered chocolate between us.

This isn't about Will. It's not about Wade.

It's about me. My goals. My business. My life.

"It's okay," I say genuinely. "That was sweet. But I'm not ready for anything. Not like that."

"I know," he says softly. "You already told me. I just got caught up. High school crushes don't die easy, I guess."

"Wait—*you* had a crush on *me*?"

"Beth, everyone did. You were terrifying. In a good way."

I grin. "You're not making a great case for yourself."

"Good. I'll stick to the friend lane." He holds up a hand. "On one condition."

"Here we go..."

"Come line dancing with me next Wednesday. Platonically. I just need a wingperson with rhythm."

I consider. Honestly, I haven't danced since the concert and it sounds like just the medicine I need.

"No kisses?" I raise an eyebrow.

"Cross my heart!" And he does.

"Deal," I say, shaking his hand.

He pulls back, then gasps. "Wait! One more condition."

"Yes?"

"Help me finish this dessert before I explode."

I raise my fork. "Now *that* I can do."

Thirty-One

It's Not a Date

Beth

Wade and I have already been at the Nashville Club for about an hour when I spot Jane across the room. She's all dolled up—hair curled and spilling out of a wicker hat, tight jeans, and a black tank top that cuts off just above her belly button. It's supposed to be a casual night out with friends, but she looks dressed to impress. Chuck, no doubt. They've been going strong for over a month now.

I touch Wade's chest lightly. "Excuse me one sec. Jane's finally here!"

He leans in, breath warm against my ear. "Your friends always run late, or are they just dramatic?"

I smirk. "Definitely dramatic. But Jane's worth it."

"So are you," he says with a wink, then spins me into a sloppy half-turn and back into his arms, laughing. "See? You're starting to get it!"

He's charming—I'll give him that. But the compliment misses its mark. I'm just not in the market.

I move toward Jane, Wade close on my heels.

"Hey, Jane!" I call out. "'Bout time you got here! I've been making a royal fool of myself without you."

"I thought you brought Wade," Jane says.

Does she look relieved?

"I did." I gesture with my thumb over my shoulder. He steps up beside me and slides a hand around my waist.

"Oooh," Jane draws the word out, then pulls me aside as she moves further into the bar. "Okay, so look—I didn't know he was coming or I would've warned you. He was pulling into the parking lot just as we were, and Chuck said he *maaaaay* have invited him."

"What are you talking about?" I ask, then look past Chuck and see him.

Will.

My heart leaps straight into my throat, and I cough.

Has he always looked this good? Of course he has. That's his thing.

I take a breath, trying to center myself. Will is here. So what? I'm out with friends, learning to line dance, enjoying a few drinks. I can smile. I can be polite.

"You okay?" Wade asks, following my gaze. When he spots Will, his jaw tightens.

"Oh. *Him.*" He takes a slow sip of his drink, like it might help him swallow whatever bitter thing he wants to say. "Didn't think this was his scene."

"It's a public dance hall," I mutter. "Anyone can come."

"Just saying." He pulls me in a little closer. "You sure you don't want me to keep you distracted?"

Before I can answer, Jane cuts in. "I'm sorry. I know how you feel about him. I really should have warned you."

"No, no, I'm fine." I step out of Wade's arms and wave her off. "He's really not that bad once you get to know him. And I've got Wade as backup if I need it, so I'm good."

Wade smiles proudly, stepping fully into the role of knight in shining armor. It's meant to be sweet, I guess—but it feels more like possession than protection.

"Yay! I'm so glad. Whatever he said to you at Chuck's party had you really bummed for, like, the rest of the night. I was worried!"

"It was just a simple misunderstanding," I insist. "No big deal. Come on,

I'll show you to the table."

Of course it *was* a big deal. But I'm an adult—I can handle it.

As both Will and Wade approach the table, I question that assessment.

Introductions go smoothly enough. Will greets me, and I greet him back, asking how his trip went. All is well until he turns to Wade.

"Wade," Will says with the kind of calm that seems practiced. He extends a hand.

Wade scoffs. "I don't shake hands with snakes."

A flicker of tension sparks in Will's eyes, but it vanishes almost instantly.

"That's a shame," he says evenly, dropping his hand. "Would've been your only shot at winning tonight."

"What's that supposed to mean?" Wade straightens, shoulders tightening.

Will just smiles—that slow, infuriating kind of smile that makes you question whether you're losing a competition you didn't even know you were in.

Jane, looking completely out of her depth, jumps in. "I'm gonna grab a few drinks. Anyone want anything?"

"Just a water for me." I gesture to my half-full lemon drop.

"Nah, I'm good," Wade huffs, glaring at Will, who pretends not to notice.

"You know what I like," Chuck adds, draping his jacket over a chair.

"I'll get a drink," Will says, like nothing happened, and follows Jane toward the bar.

Wade watches him go with narrowed eyes. "You sure you know who that guy really is?"

I shrug.

Well. That went well.

I take the opportunity to excuse myself to the dance floor. Will doesn't dance. I should be safe there.

I insert myself at the end of one of the lines of dancers, dutifully trying to follow the steps. I'm doing alright, as long as I keep my eyes glued to the feet ahead of me—they clearly know what they're doing. I've almost got the first eight steps down when a very familiar pair of jeans and boots comes into my peripheral vision.

My eyes follow them up.

There go all eight steps.

I stumble, stepping left while everyone else steps right, and find myself bumping into a very solid shoulder. He smells like clean laundry and... dreams.

"Hi, Will," I say, as casually as I can manage. "Sorry. I'm no good at this."

"Neither am I," he laughs. "So we shall both look silly." He gives a courtly bow and falls into step beside me.

Levity looks good on him. Texas seems to have done him some good. I mean to say something more, but the rest of the floor doesn't stop for our reunion. A pivot turns the whole line ninety degrees—except Will and me.

I shuffle my feet into position, facing the right direction now, with Will behind me. I try to recenter.

Forget he's there. Focus on the moves. Forget that he's—

"Oof!" I bump into a man in his fifties—pressed flannel, Wranglers, neatly trimmed mustache.

"Sorry," I cringe.

"You're fine," he says with a kind smile. "Keep at it. You'll get it."

He stomps a boot, lifts a knee, and—of course—we're turning again.

Now I'm side-by-side with Will, facing the back of the dance hall. "What's wrong with looking a little silly?" I ask as I grapevine in the opposite direction and clap on beat with the rest of the room.

Nailed it!

"Nothing at all," he says, his voice easy and warm. "I'm enjoying this."

"Oh, are you?" I laugh. He's always been the one to take himself seriously—always curated, composed.

He missteps. I flub a heel-toe. And somehow, that's all it takes. We're laughing, stumbling through one song after another, arms brushing, breath short.

There's no space for small talk—but plenty for quick jokes and glances that last just a little too long.

At one point, Jane and Chuck pull up beside us, showing off their moves.

"How? When?" I gasp. "Jane! Look at you bustin' a move!"

She laughs, keeping perfect time. "Dance teacher, remember? Besides, we've been taking lessons at the community center. Every Tuesday and Thursday."

"Yeah," Chuck adds, "and practicing in my kitchen."

Jane blushes. Chuck grins. I raise a salacious eyebrow at both of them.

"And right foot stomp and left foot stomp," Jane instructs, her voice sliding easily into teacher mode.

Will and I glance at each other and follow along.

Then I catch sight of Wade.

He's leaning against the high-top table, arms crossed. Not dancing. Not smiling. Just watching.

The song ends, and the next is a partner dance—a two-step. I turn to leave the floor and make space for couples.

Will holds out his hand as I pass.

"Shall we?"

Thirty-Two

Dirty Dancing

Beth

His eyes are so damn charming, and his smile is gentler than I remember. Add in the black button-down with the top two buttons undone, revealing just enough smooth chest to make me stupid—and yeah. My mind goes straight to the night we shared. And my body? Follows like it has no self-control at all.

Heat shoots through me, and without thinking, I take his hand.

Chuck sweeps Jane gracefully across the floor, leaving me alone—arm in arm with the most beguiling, confusing, infuriating, sexy man in the universe.

Thanks a lot, Jane.

I'm suddenly *very* aware of Will's hand as it guides and sways with mine. Sometimes he pulls in when I should be spinning out, or I bring the wrong foot forward and we collide. It should be a mess—and yet, we laugh. We try again. And somehow, we start to find a rhythm. If I didn't know better, I'd say we're actually starting to dance.

Partner dancing in a country bar is kind of like swing or ballroom—there's supposed to be this pragmatic little space between you, this polite buffer.

But the longer we move together, the smaller that space gets.

When he turns me and I land with my back against his chest, we should barely touch. But I feel all of him. His hand finds my hip and pulls me closer—closer than is strictly allowed in any respectable two-step.

A few more twirls, and this time, when he brings me back in, we're face to face. His hand finds my shoulder, then wraps around it. My breath catches. I forget the steps. We're just swaying now, like we're slow dancing at a high school prom.

"Hey," I say, meeting his eyes.

"Hey," he says back.

I focus on his lips. I remember the way they felt on mine, on my skin. The memory rolls through me in a slow, molten wave. When he draws in a breath, I wonder if he's thinking about the same thing.

"Thank you for the gifts," he says softly.

The words tug me back to the surface. I blink. I've looked up the deeds. I know Wade was right. And yet, here I am, swaying in his arms like that knowledge doesn't matter. I take a deep breath, trying to shake off the heat curling around my spine.

"Yeah, um..." Think, Beth. *Think*. "You're welcome. Did Gia like hers?" Of course I know she did; she told me herself.

My weak deflection doesn't work. He nods. "She did. So did I."

"I'm glad to hear it," I manage, even though every rational thought in my head is losing a battle to everything *else* happening inside me.

We're now ear to ear. His breath is warm against my neck. I feel it—short, quick. Mine mirrors his. I picture his lips there. On my neck. Then higher.

I picture undressing him. Taking him home. Letting it all unravel, again.

My whole body lights up.

But then the song ends. And slowly, the space between us begins to widen. He keeps holding my hand. But I feel the shift.

"You okay?" he asks.

"I could use a little fresh air," I say, breathless, a little lightheaded. Where are my smelling salts when I need them?

He squeezes my hand gently. "I could too. Follow me."

I don't let go of his hand as he weaves us through the dance floor toward the exit.

"Hey!" Wade's voice cuts through the music. I turn, startled. He stands with his arms crossed, eyes narrowed. "I thought you were here with *me* tonight."

"I was. I am." My mind spins while the thought of Will's lips lingers behind my eyes. "Just going out for some… air."

"Whatever." He throws his arms up and turns back toward the floor.

Will shakes his head, chuckling under his breath. "Come on."

I laugh too. Wade had spent most of the night dancing solo or showing me how *not* to step on my own feet. It was friendly. Platonic. But apparently the "just friends" clause expired the second Will walked in.

I shrug it off. My mind is focused on more important things. Namely: Will. Alone. Possibly shirtless.

We step past the doorwoman, down a short hallway, and out into the chilly spring air.

"Ahh! That feels good," I exclaim as the breeze hits my flushed cheeks.

Will doesn't say anything. He just leads me along the side of the building, away from the crowd, away from the lights. When we turn the corner, he spins me around—*surprisingly deftly*—and I land right back in his arms.

We kiss. Slow this time. Sweet.

He tastes like whiskey- warm with a little spice.

I pull him closer, wanting to devour him, right there in the shadows. But I stop myself. I breathe. I savor.

His hands come up to cradle my face, holding me gently, lips brushing, then pressing, then deepening. There's a storm beneath every kiss, held just barely at bay. And I let myself feel all of it.

Then he pulls back and hugs me. Full body. Heart to heart, like he means it.

I press into him, feeling how hard his heart is pounding.

I lift my face, kiss his neck, his jaw, then his lips again—slow, easy, warm, steady.

He whispers against my lips, "I think I'm in love with you."

I want to say it back.

I do.

I think I love you, too.

But the words catch in my throat. My body says yes. My heart wants to believe. But my mind… my mind won't let go.

What comes out instead surprises us both.

"I saw the deed."

Oh shit. Oh fuck.

"What?" he breathes, confused, still so close.

"I saw it, Will. The deed to your ranch."

My stomach twists. My pulse thunders.

"…And?" he says slowly, squeezing his eyes shut and rubbing the bridge of his nose. He's still standing close, but I feel the space open up between us.

"And it has your name on it. Not Gia's." The words come out sharper than I intend. Accusatory. Mean. I wish I could snatch them back. But they're out now, in the air, hanging between us like smoke.

He steps back. Fully now. No more contact.

"You really do think the worst of me," he says, and his voice cuts clean.

No, I want to say. *I just don't know how to read you.*

But my mouth betrays me again. "Well, what am I supposed to think?"

He's silent. Slowly, he takes another step back. And another.

"Think whatever you want," he says at last. "I can't keep doing this. I can't keep defending myself to you."

He pauses. My chest caves.

"Good night, Beth."

He turns and walks to his truck. I stand frozen as he backs out of the lot and disappears into the night.

Eventually, I gather myself. I go back inside, eyes scanning for my purse. I skirt along the wall, avoiding Wade, Jane, and Chuck on the dance floor. I make it to the exit without being seen.

Once I'm in my car, I send them a quick group text:

Got sick. Will walked me out to my car. Headed home. Sry guys.

Only then do I let myself cry.

This isn't how I wanted the night to end, but maybe it's how it needed to.

Thirty-Three

So Done

Will

Anger rides shotgun as I pull out of the parking lot. Every time I get close to Beth, she finds something to blame me for. It's like I can't win. So why even bother?

I huff and crank up the music.

The night had gone well—or so I thought. I joined Jane and Chuck to get out of my comfort zone, to do something completely uncomfortable: publicly proving I have no rhythm. And yet... I actually enjoyed it.

Wade was an unpleasant surprise. But I played it cool, pretended he didn't get to me—even when every inch of my skin itched to knock the smug right off his face. But Beth... seeing her happy, laughing, dancing without caring how she looked? That made Wade's presence bearable.

She made missing steps and forgetting the count easy. Because with her in the room, I didn't care what anyone else thought.

And that's the problem, isn't it? I care way too damn much what that insufferable woman thinks about me.

The music cuts out as my Bluetooth flashes an incoming call. Chuck.

I answer, trying to keep my voice even. "Hey, man. Sorry to bail on you."

"No worries, bro. Just calling to check on Beth. You—wait—you bailed?" His voice strains over the background din of the club.

"She's not there with you?" I ask, that knot of worry rising faster than I expect.

"Wait, one sec. I can barely hear you!"

I hear shuffling, a muffled shout, then the line clears.

"Okay, better. What'd you say?"

I repeat the question.

"Oh. No. Beth said she was sick and heading home. Said you walked her out to her car, so I figured I'd just check in. You gone too?"

I don't even feel bad. She wasn't sick. She was pissed. Probably off somewhere pouting because she didn't get her full pound of flesh.

"Yeah," I say. "I actually left before Beth did. I thought she was still there. Did you try calling her?"

"Jane is right now. Figured I'd try you at the same time. What happened between you two?"

"She's so fucking stubborn," I snap.

"She's what, now?"

"She thinks she knows everything about me, but she won't take five minutes to actually *ask*. She just... decides who I am and then punishes me for it." I grip the wheel tighter. "I'm tired of being on trial with her."

There's a pause on the other end.

"Oookay. I'll bite. What happened?"

"I guess she went digging around and found out the ranch deed is in my name. And yeah, it is. *It has to be.* Gia can't use her inheritance or legally own property until she's eighteen. She *knows* that. But Beth—" I shake my head, fuming— "Beth acted like I'd swindled Gia. Like I'm some con artist pretending to be noble. Shit, she sounded just like Wade. I bet he got to her."

The words leave my mouth before I can stop them. And now I'm seething.

Fuck Wade.

Chuck's voice cuts in, calm and maddening. "Have you tried just... telling her the truth?"

I nearly bark a laugh. "I shouldn't *have to*!"

"You *shouldn't have to...*" He repeats my words like he's trying them on for size.

"She gets these ideas in her head, and then I have to prove I'm not whatever guy she's decided I am. I'm tired of defending myself for things I haven't even done."

Chuck sighs. "Whoa, slow your roll. What do you mean you *shouldn't have to?* Of course you do. That's how people get to know you. You *tell them*. Have you actually told Beth anything real about yourself?"

I want to snap back, but... grilled cheese and that conversation at the coffee shop is about all I've given her. That—and the parts she's had to piece together on her own.

"Course I have," I say, but I don't sound convinced. "But I shouldn't have to lay out my whole life story for her to give me the benefit of the doubt by now."

Chuck's quiet for a beat. Then he says, "Has Beth ever told you why she came back?"

I rub my face with one hand as I drive. "Something about a change of pace. Couldn't handle the city, I suppose."

"Her ex cheated on her."

That stops me. "Oh?"

"She was with him for years. Joint savings account—one he controlled. Turns out, he'd been siphoning money for *two years* and seeing other people. When everything came out, he moved out, leaving her stuck with a lease she couldn't afford and barely any of the emergency fund she thought they had."

"Why didn't she take him to court?" I'm stunned. Beth doesn't seem like the type to let someone get away with that.

"With what money?" Chuck asks. "He could afford a lawyer. She couldn't. And even if she sued, the account was in his name. She was just listed as an emergency contact or something—never actually had control of the funds."

My stomach twists.

Chuck continues, his voice protective. "She thought she was going to marry that guy. And he burned her. Bad. That's what she came back from."

A part of me softens. I feel it—a stab of sympathy. But another part digs in.

"Then why didn't she *tell* me that?"

I hear Chuck's intake of breath. Then, "I'm going to tell you something, friend. And I'm only saying it because I love you and you need to hear it."

He pauses, lets it land.

"You are so damned *prideful*, Will."

The words echo but refuse to sink in.

"What the hell do you mean? I haven't lied to her. I shouldn't have to bear the weight of another man's bullshit."

Chuck's tone hardens. "Prideful. Not deceitful. You care way too much what people think. When someone sees you wrong, you put up a wall and let them stay wrong. You think your reputation should speak for itself—and maybe it does, back on the East Coast. But not here."

He hesitates, giving me a moment to absorb it.

"Beth likes you, man. Enough to keep trying. Enough to keep *hoping* she's wrong. Maybe stop playing this love-hate game and actually *talk to her.*"

I don't answer. I'm still mad. And hurt. And, yeah, maybe a little ashamed.

Chuck's voice cuts in again. "Jane's walking back. I'mma go see if she reached Beth. Just… drop the righteous indignation. Tell her the truth. I'll talk to you later."

He hangs up.

But his words hang in the air like a damn sermon I can't shake.

Maybe he's right. Maybe I need to lay it all out, no armor, no games. And if she still rejects me then at least I'll know I did my part. That she said no to *me*, not just the version of me Wade or her ex painted in her head.

Still… I'm not doing it face to face. I can't.

As I drive, I try to think of what I'd say in a message, but it all jumbles. Too much. Too complicated. A text feels cheap. An email feels cold. A letter?

Too old-fashioned.

Then I remember the journal. The one Beth gave me. She said it was for writing letters to my parents. I remember her sweetly scrawled note.

Maybe a letter isn't so old-fashioned after all.

Thirty-Four

Puppy Love

Beth

It's Sunday afternoon, and I'm in the backyard tossing a tennis ball for Bowie, watching him bound through the grass like he's been training for a puppy Olympics. The sun is warm on my shoulders, the scent of sage and fresh-cut grass in the air. Every time he returns with the ball, his tail wags so hard it throws off his balance.

"Okay, sit," I say, holding the ball high. He plants his butt instantly, tongue lolling out, ears alert.

"Good boy!" I toss the ball again, and he bolts after it like it's a national emergency.

I can't stop smiling. My whole body feels lighter when I'm with him—like this weird little dog has wiggled his way into the corners of my life I didn't even realize were empty.

I check the time. I've got the convention tomorrow—the clinical psychology session on the therapeutic potential of DMT in trauma recovery. I've been looking forward to it for weeks. It's a full-day event in Reno, and a good change of pace and scenery.

My phone buzzes with an incoming text from Jane.

hate to do this but I can't watch Bowie tomorrow. Sarah sick - teaching her classes.

I tap out that its no big deal and I hope she feels better, even as my mind goes to work looking for solutions.

She replies with a heart emoji, and that's that.

I glance down at Bowie, who's now nose-deep in a bush, tail wagging like mad.

"What am I going to do with you?"

I mentally scroll my list.

Mom and Dad – Out of town, enjoying retired life.

Carol – Has therapy clients. Horses. Chaos. Not happening.

Chuck – Too high-speed. Probably in three places at once.

Cassie – Works the lunch shift at Overland.

My phone dings again then again They're both from Gia.

I wrote Mom tday so gooooood ♥

when do I get 2 c puppy???????

Below it, a gif of a cartoon bunny with giant watery eyes, pops in, just begging for love.

Damn. I'd meant to introduce Bowie to Gia after they got back from Texas, but then *everything* happened with Will... and I just couldn't bring myself to reach out.

Not because of Gia. She didn't do anything wrong.

It's Will. I keep wondering if maybe I owe him an apology—but for what? For pointing out the truth? For *asking* a question?

Still... avoiding her isn't fair. She's just a kid. And she deserves better than to be caught in the crossfire of my mess with her brother.

I hesitate, then tap out a message before I overthink it.

Actually, how'd you like to watch him for the day? My sitter bailed and I have to be in Reno early. I'll even pay you!

Gia's response comes so quickly I wonder how she managed it:

yes yes yes yes yes yes yes yes yes yes yes yes yes yes yes yes yes yes yes yes yes

I hesitate, feeling awkward

Did you ask Will? Make sure he's okay with it.
I don't feel like dealing with him directly. She's fourteen. She can ask.
A moment later:
he good w it 👍
I exhale.

Two nights ago, I somehow managed to offend Will *again*, and now I'm dropping my dog off at his house like we're on speaking terms. What even *is* my life?

"Come on, Bowie," I say, clipping his leash back on. "Let's go pick up Gamma Missy from getting her hair all did."

* * *

When I pull into the Fitzgerald Ranch driveway, my stomach flips. No sign of Will's giant red truck. *Thank God.*

I park, and before I can even grab Bowie's leash, Gia's running down the steps, full sprint.

As soon as I cut the engine, she flings open the passenger door.

"Oh my *gaaaawd!*" she squeals. "You're so *cute!*"

Her voice pitches high enough to summon wildlife. Bowie leaps out, tail wagging like a propeller, and she drops into a crouch, letting him climb all over her.

I grab his tote and leash, following her into the house.

"Where's your brother?" I ask, casually as I can manage.

"Out back, changing the oil on his truck." She waves a hand toward the rear of the house.

"Cool." I blow out a quiet breath.

I set the bag on the counter. "He's been fed, but I brought treats if you want to try some training. There's a chew stick in there too."

"Oh, he won't be bored," Gia coos into Bowie's snout. "Will he, baby? No, he will not!"

I laugh. "Okay, I've got to get on the road, but—"

The back door creaks open.

"Beth?"

Shit. Bad idea. Abort mission.

I pivot to make a rapid exit. "Yeah, hey!" I call out. "Sorry, can't stay to chat, but thank you for letting Gia help me out!"

"Huh?" Will walks in, wiping grease off his hands with a rag. He looks... flustered.

Gia pipes up. "Um, yeah, so this is Bowie and—"

Will lifts an eyebrow. "First stuffed animals, now real ones?"

I resist the urge to roll my eyes. "This one's mine. I thought you were okay with her watching him for the day."

Will glances at Gia, who just shrugs. "I figured it was easier to ask forgiveness than permission. *Look at him*, Will. Isn't he the cutest thing you've ever seen?"

I edge closer to the door. "Sorry. She said you were okay with it."

He looks surprised. Uncertain. But then a small smile touches his lips. "What's his name?"

So the man has a soft spot for dogs. And can change his own oil. *Of course he does.*

"Bowie," Gia and I say at the same time.

"Is it okay?" I ask. "I have to be on the road like five minutes ago. She's really saving my ass."

He hesitates, then nods. "It's okay."

Good enough.

I make my escape.

I'm halfway down the steps when he calls after me.

"Wait, before you go—"

I stop. He's already jogging down to meet me.

"I have something for you," he says. He looks more nervous than I've ever seen him. "To read. Or look at. Just... take it."

He holds out an envelope. His eyes are downcast, and that throws me more than anything else.

"I really can't. I have to be in Reno by 9:30 and—" I gesture uselessly. I start backing toward my car.

"You don't have to read it now," he says quickly, walking beside me. "Just… please take it. It would mean a lot."

I don't want to, but I take it. He places it in my hand gently, like it's breakable.

"It's nothing bad. Cross my heart."

He walks back toward the house before I can say anything else.

I slide into the driver's seat, toss the envelope onto the passenger side, and pull out of the driveway for the hour-long drive of:

What the actual hell just happened?

Thirty-Five

No More Games

~ॐ~

Beth

"Uno!" I shout, slapping down a green four.

Bowie barks once, wagging his tail and pushing his nose into my hand like I've just barked an ancient doggy summoning spell.

"Ahh," Chuck sighs dramatically. "Then I guess I have no choice but to play this." He tosses down a card that reverses the order *and* makes me draw four.

"I swear," I grumble, picking up my cards. "You've got a dark side."

Dad chuckles as he pulls seven cards from the draw pile before finally slapping down a yellow. "Finally," he mutters.

I let out a wicked cackle. "Draw those cards, old man! No mercy."

He's still sun-kissed from backpacking in Yosemite, so I don't feel bad at all. *Uno: No Mercy* lives up to its name—especially in this house.

"So…" Mom's voice cuts in, all syrup and subtlety. I freeze. I know that tone. It's her patented game-night meddle cue.

"I haven't heard you mention Will. Or—what's the other guy's name?"

"Wade?" Jane offers.

"Yeah, him. How are things going with *him*?"

I roll my eyes and toss out a skip. "Nothing's going with *anyone*. I've officially sworn off men for at least the next two eternities."

Mom tuts softly, like I've just told her I'm giving up vegetables. "What was wrong with Wade? He seemed like such a nice man."

Chuck lets out a short bark of laughter. "Wade? Beth can do way better."

Mom looks confused. "Why? What's wrong with him?"

I lean back in my chair, eyeing my cards, trying *not* to join the conversation. Not my circus, not tonight.

Chuck shrugs. "His agent's an old buddy of mine. We had lunch last week—he said Wade wanted the Silver Sage Ranch, badly."

"Then Will swooped in and nabbed it," I mumble, my stomach giving a familiar twist.

Oops. So much for not participating.

Chuck shakes his head. "That's not exactly how it went down. Wade tried to put offers in for weeks, but couldn't lock in financing. Dropped out of escrow twice."

"Huh." It's all I manage. One syllable, heavy with implications.

"Yeah, but what about the deed?" Jane presses. "Wade wasn't wrong about that."

"Have you talked to Will about it?" Chuck asks, suddenly serious, looking over his bright Uno hand.

"Uh... no," I admit.

"You mean *he* hasn't talked to *you*?" His voice drops, more disappointed than judgmental.

I hesitate. "He did give me a letter."

"And?" Mom's voice is too quick.

"And I haven't read it yet." I toss a blue skip into the pile. "Sorry, Dad."

He groans. "Unforgivable."

Chuck shifts in his seat, more thoughtful now. "Look, I don't want to speak out of turn, but... I think Will deserves a chance to speak for himself. As far as the deed goes, he did everything in his power to put it in Gia's name. But the judge said no—it was too risky for a minor. So Will used his own money."

"And when Gia turns eighteen… what, it just transfers to her?" I ask, skeptical.

"Exactly. There's a contract in place. The deed goes to her, no strings."

I blink, processing. "So he just bought her a whole-ass ranch."

Chuck nods. "Basically, yeah."

There's a pause—one of those thick, contemplative family silences—and then Jane plays her card.

"How about we talk about something more important?" she says with feigned sweetness. "Like… this plus ten."

She lays it down with the innocence of a saint. *Diabolical.*

Chuck groans so loud even Bowie perks up. "That's it. I'm calling your mother."

I laugh, but my brain's already spinning. Will has ping-ponged in my head from angel to devil and back so many times I can't keep score.

By the time Chuck finishes picking up ten cards, the conversation shifts—thankfully—to something less emotionally treacherous. When Jane eventually wins, I excuse myself, citing an early morning and a pounding sugar crash.

I hug Dad first, then Mom. She holds on a moment longer than usual.

"You know," she says gently, "I don't pry to be nosy. I just want to see you happy."

I nod. "I know you care, Mom. Right now, I just need to focus on taking care of me."

She pulls back slightly. "That's all a mom really wants—the well-being of her children."

"Thanks, Mom." I press a kiss to her cheek.

As I hug Chuck, he puts his hands on my shoulders and meets my eyes. "Maybe you should read the letter."

I nod.

Thirty-Six

The Letter

Beth

I curl beneath my quilted comforter, arms cocooned in soft cotton, the quiet of the room humming like a lullaby around me. Bowie lies at my feet, curled in a loose cinnamon bun of warmth and fur, his tiny snores making my heart ache in the best way.

Outside, I can see tree branches move in the summer wind, but inside my room, all is still. Bowie shifts and kicks as he chases dream lizards. Maybe not entirely still.

I stare at the ceiling, tracing the faint peaks of the popcorn spackle while my thoughts tangle themselves around one man.

Will.

I keep thinking I've got him figured out. Then something shifts, and the picture morphs again. At first, I thought he was a polished, arrogant control freak. Then maybe he was sweet—but misleading. Then maybe he was selfless. Or maybe he was just good at pretending.

Wade certainly wasn't a reliable witness. And the deed, well… it might not be what it seemed either. Chuck's version of the story sits heavy in my chest.

Everything I thought I knew keeps flipping upside down.

I could write Will off as one of life's great unsolved mysteries, but that's not the truth. Not really.

The truth is: just thinking about him makes my skin tingle.

My stomach flips as my hand absently traces the line of my abdomen, like it's remembering his touch all on its own. I pull my hand back, muttering under my breath.

"Stop it. Beth. Don't go there."

Bowie shifts, lifting his head briefly to look at me. His ears twitch as if to say *well, you were thinking really loud,* then he sighs and nestles deeper into the blanket at my feet.

I glance at the envelope on my bedside table.

It's been sitting there for days, practically humming. Chuck's words ring in my ears—*maybe you should read the letter.*

I know I should. But every time I look at it, my heart beats faster. My palms go clammy.

What if it's full of accusations? Or guilt trips? What if he lists every single way I've been unfair to him?

I reach for the envelope anyway.

The paper is thick, folded with care. His handwriting is clean and slanted, a little stiff, like he tried too hard to make it neat.

My hands tremble slightly as I open the letter.

Beth,

I'm not great at letters. Or, apparently, at saying the right thing when it counts. But I wanted you to hear this from me without me messing it up in person.

You were right about one thing: I've made mistakes. But taking Gia's inheritance or cutting her out of her own dream isn't one of them. The ranch is hers—I'm just holding it until she's old enough to sign her own name.

I know I've given you every reason to doubt me. And maybe I should've fought harder to prove you wrong instead of just hoping you'd see through the noise. That's on me.

I don't expect you to trust me yet. I just don't want you to keep trusting the version of me that isn't real.

I'd like the chance to let you get to know me. No stories. No charm. Just me.

—Will

P.S. Tell Bowie I said thanks for being such an affectionate supportive man to the women I love. Maybe one day I'll be as good as he is, minus the face licks.

I blink once, then again. I reread the postscript, over and over.

The women I love.

That's twice now.

I don't know what I expected. Something defensive, maybe. A list of justifications. But this… this is just a man laying himself bare.

My chest rises and falls as I drop the hand holding the paper onto my legs, hearing the faint crumple of the paper edges.

I close my eyes.

If he were here right now, sitting beside me, would I argue? Demand more proof?

Or would I straddle him and cover him in kisses until he couldn't breathe?

I lift a hand, brushing my fingertips lightly across my lips.

I don't know if I love him. Not yet.

But I think it's time to stop holding so tightly to my suspicion. Time to stop waiting for him to disappoint me. Time to give him a real chance.

I glance at Bowie.

He wags his tail in his sleep.

"Don't worry boy," I whisper, grinning faintly. "You're still the best man in the house."

He lets out a sleepy snuffle, and I settle deeper under the covers, Will's letter still pinched in my fingers.

Thirty-Seven

Broken Fences

Beth

The alarm I wake up to can't be mine.

Mine is a gentle composition of piano and strings. This is sharp and grating like my phone ringer. It takes me a heartbeat to realize it is.

By the time I fumble for my phone, I've missed the call. It was Carol.

I blink as my eyes struggle to focus on the time.

4:17 AM.

I call her back but it goes straight to voicemail.

I toss my warm, snugly comforter off to the side and pull myself to sitting. Whatever it is, I'm up.

When I call again, she answers on the second ring.

"Beth! Sorry to wake you. The wind knocked a section of the fence loose. The horses got out."

"All of them?"

"I've got Pepper and Maple secured, but Cocoa and Biscuit are still missing."

"I'm on the way."

I throw on pants, a sweater, and socks then dig through the closet for my winter jacket. My breath fogs the window as I check outside. The wind hasn't stopped all night. Its dry, but sharp and relentless.

By the time I step into the hallway, Dad's already up, buttoning his flannel. "Grab the Maglites," Mom calls from the front of the house.

"Already on it," he says, opening the hall closet. He hands me one of the heavy black flashlights, and I grip it like a weapon.

Down the hall, I find Mom already pouring coffee into two travel mugs. "The weather spares no one," she says gently, taking it in the kind of stride that comes with growing up in the Valley.

Dad's at the door, boots half-laced. "Chuck just called. He's up. We're meeting at Carol's."

I take the mug Mom hands me. "Thanks." I shiver, still trying to work the last bit of sleep off.

She squeezes my arm and offers a warm, no-nonsense look. "You'll find them."

The sky is still navy blue when we jump into Dad's truck. Patches of dry sagebrush, and the silver glow of early dawn press at the edges of the valley.

The drive is short but tense. We can feel the gusts against our truck and see it, as dust, leaves, and occasional debris swirl past our headlights. Giant tumbleweeds bounce and roll, loosened from their weak grasp of the earth. Dad doesn't slow for them, so when he intercepts one, it explodes with a dull thud, spreading broken bits along the road behind us.

When we arrive at Healing Spirit Stables, I feel the bite of the air the second I open the truck door. Cold air cuts straight through my coat and lashes my cheeks. Carol's silhouette stands near the paddock gate with Pepper and Maple secured inside. A couple of vehicles are already parked nearby—Chuck's truck, and another one I don't immediately recognize. There are half a dozen people, jackets pulled tight and beanies snug on heads, preparing to search. I see another silhouette come around the corner who turns out to be Chuck, holding a length of rope.

"The fence along the east trail went down," Carol explains. "Pepper and Hazel stayed close but the other two seemed to have wandered a bit further. Damnit, I hope they weren't too spooked or they could be anywhere in these hills!"

Sunrises and Sagebrush

She let out an exasperated sigh, but my trained eyes and ears detect a fair bit of worry.

"We'll check the ridge above the trail," Dad says.

"What happened?" I inquire.

Carol lets out a long breath. "Ooh, wouldn't you know…that old elm finally went down. It crushed half the fence." Then she mutters, more to herself than us, "Tree guy was supposed to take it out at the end of the month. Guess nature beat him to it."

More headlights appear down the drive. Within minutes our group doubles—people from the feed store, the trail club, and even one of Missy's knitting circle friends. No one needs much prompting. Some start spreading out on foot and on horseback to search. A few head to the fenceline with chainsaws and gloves.

"Take the ridge," Carol tells Dad and me. "Mike's going south. Jolene and her boys are checking the streambeds."

I follow Dad and Chuck toward the trail.

The air is still thick with dust and grit. My flashlight beam cuts across a narrow trail, but it's useless beyond a few feet. I call out softly as we move.

"Cocoa… Biscuit…" Then, I pull out the big guns, "I've got treats!"

My voice all but disappears into the wind.

We split up as the sun begins to rise, warm light spilling over the desert and casting long shadows that speckle through the sagebrush. I move toward the far side of the ridge, boots crunching over rock and dry earth. The tension in my chest hasn't eased.

Movement catches my attention and my anticipation flares, hoping it is one of the horses. It is Cocoa, and he isn't alone. He is walking nonchalantly down a path slightly parallel to my own, being led by a figure I recognize at once.

Will.

He's leading Cocoa along the narrow trail that loops behind the paddock, his head bowed slightly against the wind, his steps steady. He doesn't see me. He's focused on the horse, one hand on the lead rope, the other raised to shield his face from the gusts.

I stop, just for a second, tempted to call out.

The sight of him hits me harder than I expect. He looks so strong, capable, and at ease, which compliment's Cocoa's easy walk, like they're just two dudes out for a morning walk. The wind tosses the hem of his coat and lifts the tips of Cocoa's mane. They look like they belong out here, like they're part of this place.

I follow at a distance, watching him until we reach the stables. It's a little stalkerish, but I am captivated by his relaxed demeanor when he thinks he's alone.

Carol and Mom are waiting at the gate. Jolene and two tall, lanky teen boys arrive a few minutes later with Biscuit in tow, coaxed down from a ridge above the main pasture.

All the horses are safe. I let out a breath I hadn't realized I was holding.

"Hot coffee and donuts, coming in hot!" Missy's voice calls from the back of her 4Runner as she distributes cups, napkins, and cheerful encouragement.

"You need this," she says simply, handing me a steaming cup. "You've got that look like your bones are cold."

I laugh under my breath and take both. "Thanks, Mom."

She wraps an arm around me. "You did good this morning."

Someone sets up a folding table. Another neighbor, Hal, arrives with extra fence slats. Carol's son-in-law rolls in with a second chainsaw. The morning becomes a hive of movement—tools passed, branches hauled, jokes traded across the fence line.

No one mentions money. No one's paid. This is what people do here: they show up.

Out of the corner of my eye, I see Will crouched beside Cocoa, checking a rear hoof for stones. He moves easily, hands sure and calm. The horse trusts him. And I think for the first time, I do, too.

Carol stands beside me, sipping from her thermos. "He was the first one here," she says quietly. "Got Maple and Pepper secured before the rest of you got here."

I blink. "I didn't see his truck."

"He parked at the back gate. Brought extra halters, too." She glances at me.

"Doesn't talk much, but he gets things done."

My throat tightens and something warm blossoms inside me.

Will catches my eye just as he stands. He nods once, then gestures toward the fence line.

"Sticking around for repairs?" He asks casually.

"Yup," I say somewhat lamely, all other words cut off by the lump that just materialized in my throat.

The wind has finally started to settle, leaving behind silence and the increasing warmth of the sun.

Ahh.. the desert. So fickle.

Thirty-Eight

Mending Fences, Building Bridges

Beth

The broken fence is worse than I expected.

An entire section of rail is gone—flattened beneath the weight of a dead elm that finally gave up and collapsed in the wind. Splinters of bark and cracked limbs are scattered across the pasture like shattered bones.

Dad and Will take to the fence line, measuring out the span crushed by the fallen elm. Ben eyeballs each post location with casual authority, and Will trails him with a post hole digger slung over one shoulder, letting his sleeves roll up past his elbows as he works. His forearms are streaked with sawdust and dirt, but he doesn't seem to notice.

They don't talk much. They don't need to. Every so often, Ben gestures and Will nods, digging in without complaint.

A few yards off, I'm working with Chuck and Jolene's youngest, breaking down the branches too thick for the burn pile. We drag them to a wide circle of dirt where a bonfire is already smoldering under the supervision of Hal and a couple of his buds from the East Fork Volunteer Fire Department. I can feel the heat from the flames a few yards away as they consume the dry, brittle branches.

I watch him crouch to help Jolene's middle kid adjust the wheelbarrow he's been stubbornly dragging across the pasture. He doesn't talk down to him, just shows him how to balance the weight, then walks alongside for a few steps before returning to the fence.

He doesn't know I'm watching. That might be the most attractive part.

It's the same with everyone. A handshake for Hal. A respectful nod to Carol. A "thank you" to the high school kid who brought more screws from the truck bed. I'd seen the charming man at the coffee shop, the aloof scrooge at the concert, and now I am seeing another side of him. It's relaxed, friendly, and more attractive than I'd like it to be right now.

I toss another thick branch into the fire and glance back toward the fence. Will's kneeling now, bracing one of the new beams while Ben drills. He wipes a bead of sweat from his temple, leaving a dark streak of dirt across his cheek. I have to force myself to look away, to focus on dead branches and the roaring fire.

Just beyond the paddock, I spot another familiar figure—Wade, of all people—hauling fence rails from the back of someone's flatbed. He doesn't wave. Doesn't even look our way. Just mutters something to Hal, grabs another slat, and keeps moving.

Carol sidles up beside me, a thermos still in her hand. "Didn't expect to see Wade," she murmurs.

"Neither did I," I reply, watching him hammer a board into place with a little more force than strictly necessary.

"Heard he grumbled something about 'letting rich boys play cowboy,' but he still showed up at dawn with tools and gloves. Didn't even stop for coffee."

I nod. "Sounds about right."

Wade passes by, eyes flicking toward me for a split second. He gives the slightest of nods. Not friendly. Not hostile. Just... there.

He keeps walking, and I let him.

It's not forgiveness. But it's something close to closure.

Mom bustles nearby with two other women from her book club, all wearing matching wide-brimmed sun hats and coordinating aprons like they'd been planning this all along. They've set up a folding table at the edge of the work site, covering it with paper plates, cups, and a rotating spread of cut fruit, cookies, muffins, lemon bars, and a vat of lemonade that looks suspiciously like it has some iced tea mixed in.

"Hydrate or die-drate!" Missy calls, handing off water bottles like a battlefield medic. "Come grab a snack before you fall over!"

I toss my latest armload into the burn pile and head for the makeshift oasis. I sigh as I grab a cup of lemonade and one of her magic chocolate chip cookies. My mouth is full when I see Will crossing the yard to refill his bottle and thank her. He's not loud about it, not showy. Just sincere.

I hand him one of the cookies off the plate. "Here," I say, feeling shy, "Missy's Magical Cookies. They're the best."

He smiles and takes it from me, his fingers brushing against my own. I try not to think about whether or not they lingered for just a moment. I cough to clear the little knot of anticipation growing in my chest.

"You're good with Cocoa," I add. "I saw you out there."

His lips twitch at the corner. "Thanks. He was weary when I found him. With all the branches and corrugated steel slamming around, I can't blame him."

"He trusts you," I say, my voice softer now.

Will glances at me. "I guess I showed him he has nothing to fear."

The insinuation is not lost on me but I don't respond.

Instead, I hold a slat while he secures it in place.

"Lunch!" Carol calls from the porch, waving a dishtowel. "Come and eat before you collapse!"

Ben and Chuck head in first. Will hesitates, wiping sweat from his brow with the back of his wrist. I could cut through the silence between us like butter.

"I read the letter," I say finally.

He doesn't speak right away, just watches me. There is something about his eyes. They're soft, pleading.

"I owe you an apology," I speak slowly. "For not seeing you clearly."

He picks up the screw gun and turns toward the house. Then he smiles, a small mischievous grin.

"You know what I think?" He challenges.

I gulp as my stomach drops. "What?"

"I think the best apologies are delivered over dinner."

I raise an eyebrow. "Dinner?"

His grin remains small and devilish. "Tonight."

I wipe my hands on my jeans, heart thumping. "Okay."

Thirty-Nine

An Actual Date

Will

Beth beats me to the restaurant, which is honestly impressive given that I took a thirty-minute nap I pretended wasn't a nap.

I spot her across the room and damn near trip over my own feet.

She's cleaned up from the morning's chaos. She traded dusty jeans and an old shirt for a fresh, close-fitting spring dress, hair pulled back with a few wisps framing her face. The woman is radiant. But I'd take this version *or* the one that's mud-streaked, wind-whipped, sweat on her brow. That woman wielding a hammer beside me, shoulder brushing mine, jaw set with focus? She owns me.

She sees me and smiles. It's not a test. It's not guarded. It's just... Beth. The one I met at the coffee shop, her demeanor soft and easy.

I sit down across from her, catching the faint scent of her shampoo—citrusy and bright—and try to focus on the menu, not on how badly I want to brush my hand over her knee. Or skip dinner and get right down to devouring *her*.

"Hey," she says, voice lilting like the corner of her mouth.

"Hey," I reply. "Looks like you beat me here."

"Beauty takes time," she says, tilting her head.

I blink. "You do look gorgeous."

She laughs and leans in. "I meant *you*, silly."

Before I can recover, she winks. "But thank you."

The waitress arrives, takes our drink orders, and vanishes as quickly as she came.

Beth reaches across the table and places her hand over mine. Her touch sends a current through my whole body. I'm trying to breathe and also not say anything stupid when she opens her mouth.

"Before we get too far—"

"Beth! What a surprise."

I don't need to turn around to recognize that voice. The edge in it is as familiar as it is unwelcome.

Wade. Of course.

I already know what he's about to say, and I already know I won't like it.

He lingers between me and the bar, hat pulled low like it somehow makes him less of an ass.

Beth pulls her hand back from mine and it punches the air from my lungs.

"Hi, Wade," she says evenly.

He tips his hat at me. "Slumming it with the locals, Will?"

"Excuse me?" Beth's voice sharpens.

I'm already standing by the time he opens his mouth again.

"Seriously, Beth? You think someone like *him* wants a relationship with you? You're just another checkmark for a guy like that."

Rage tears through me, white-hot and reckless, but Beth stands first. She remains calm, poised, terrifying in her restraint.

"Can I help you with something, Wade?" she asks sweetly. The danger under it is electric.

"Yeah, you can come over to *that* table and eat with someone who actually appreciates you."

The man actually *winks*.

Beth's fingers return to my thigh. It's a jolt of contact and a message. *I got this.*

An Actual Date

I stay quiet, trusting her with this one. Maybe the boy in me just wants to see her punch a hole through this guy.

She squares her shoulders.

"Let's see," she says slowly. "Will runs multiple billion-dollar companies, cares for a teenage girl who lost her parents, helped her build a business, and still dragged himself out of bed at 3 a.m. to help fix my fence. You're right, Wade. I *should* be appreciating him."

I swallow hard. Her words hit like nothing else could. I don't breathe.

"He is enterprising off that property and you know it." Wade looks right past Beth and glares at me. I tighten my lips closed.

"He's taking all the risk and promising Gia all the reward." She explains like she's his kindergarten teacher. "And he's not the one going around trying to win women over by making others look bad."

Her hand tightens over mine.

She's *protecting me.*

I can't remember the last time someone did that.

Wade's face flushes dark. "Fine. You want to be his piece of meat, be my guest."

Beth doesn't even blink. "Actually, I think I do."

She steps backward into my arms, and I wrap them around her—not to shield her, not to show off. Just because it feels right. She *fits.*

"Now, if you'll excuse us," she adds, voice syrupy and dangerous, "if he's half as playful with his *meat* as I'm hoping, I'll need the calories."

I almost choke. Wade turns purple. I don't even have time to respond before he mutters, "Fucking whore."

I move then, ready to throw hands. But Beth spins around, presses her face to mine, and whispers:

"Let him show his weakness. You have nothing to prove to him."

It lands harder than any punch would've. I stop. I breathe.

She kisses me—quick, warm, and full of meaning. I return it lightly, matching her restraint.

We sit back down as the heat simmers between us.

"Sooo," she says, dragging the word, her tone light but intimate. "As I was saying before we were *so rudely interrupted...*"

I smirk.

"I read your letter."

I sip my beer, trying not to look desperate. "What'd you think?"

"It was sweet. And awkward. And dorky." She pauses for longer than is comfortable for me. That infernal woman. "And I loved it."

I laugh, exhaling tension I didn't even know I was still holding. "I felt like an idiot writing it."

"It was vulnerable, which is so much better than any amount of charm."

She looks down at the table, then back up.

"I've been working on actually seeing you. Letting your words and behavior speak instead of my fears."

"I gave you reasons to doubt me," I admit.

She shakes her head. "Not as many as you think."

A pause.

Then, softer, "Do you want to know why I really came back home?"

I nod. I already know the basics from Chuck, but I want to hear it from her.

The waitress comes and takes our order. Beth waits until she's gone before telling me everything—about her ex, the money, the way it all unraveled beneath her feet.

Her voice doesn't shake. But her eyes do and she dabs them with the edge of her cloth napkin more than once.

I want to reach across the table and hold her. Shield her. Burn the man who hurt her to the ground. Instead, I listen.

When she finishes, I lean in.

"I get it. I understand why trusting anyone—especially me—feels like stepping off a ledge. I'm not asking for a free pass. I'm asking for a chance to earn it."

She smiles, and her tears fall. She lets them. "These are good tears," she insists with a giggle that eats at every fiber of my being. .

I take her hand and kiss her knuckles. Her fingers linger in mine even after.

Dinner arrives, and we fall into a rhythm again—talking, teasing, brushing fingers over utensils. It's like that first day at the coffee shop all over again. Its so natural and easy I find myself opening up to her about my own family drama. About the veiled threats and the estate traps. I tell her everything—not for sympathy, but so she has the opportunity to know the real me, the parts of me I hide from the public eye.

When she flags down the waitress for dessert, I feel myself tighten, recalling her words to Wade.

She orders the brownie skillet. I grin.

"Good choice. I was hoping you'd get that."

"Had to," she says. "I've got calories to replace."

The words make me laugh harder than they should. "Yeah, it was a hard day."

I force myself to calm down, but the arousal lingers.

As the waitress walks away, I glance at the time. Then I rub the back of my neck.

"I, uh... I'm sorry I cut out so fast last time we were...alone together. I want to do better. I promised Gia I'd bring her a burger and watch a movie with her tonight. I didn't plan on..." I gesture between us.

Beth's eyes soften. "You don't have to explain. She's your priority. I get it."

"She is," I say. "But... that doesn't mean I want this to end."

She nods thoughtfully, then says, "Gia'll love the chicken sandwich. Get her the sweet potato fries. Trust me."

I laugh. "You're probably right."

Then, I look at her. "You could join us. No pressure. We're just watching a movie, hanging out, so no shenanigans."

"No shenanigans?" she teases and I want to take it all back.

I want to get into all the shenanigans I can with her. But Gia is my focus right now so against body, mind, and the ache between my legs, I say, "Not with a teenager between us."

She smiles slowly. "Sounds like a date."

I raise my brows. "Like a date date?"

"Maybe," she says. "Possibly. Almost definitely more than friends."

I feel the grin spread across my face, warm and unshakable.

"Then I'll get her two sandwiches. Just in case you stay long enough to want one too."

Forty

Stealth is My Talent

Will

Beth follows me in her car as I pull up to the house. My pulse is still riding high from dinner, from that kiss in the parking lot, from the way she said "maybe more than friends" like it was the simplest thing in the world and also the bravest.

I glance at her in my rearview mirror as she parks. She doesn't get out right away.

I open my door, step into the cool night air, and walk toward her slowly. She's gripping the wheel, brows drawn tight.

I pull her door open. "You okay?" I ask gently.

She turns to me, forcing a smile. "Yeah. I just… I don't want to intrude. You and Gia have your thing. I don't want to step on your space."

My heart twists.

"You're not," I say, pulling my phone from my pocket. "Hang on."

I call Gia and hit speaker. Beth draws her lips inward, waiting.

"Hey, you still alive?" I ask when she picks up.

"Duh," Gia replies. "Did you get my burger?"

"Beth recommended a chicken sandwich she thinks you'll like. And sweet potato fries."

"Sick!" Gia says, but I continue.

"Quick question—is it okay with you if Beth comes to hang out for the movie?"

"YES!" she practically shouts. "Wait, she's there now? Bring her in! I want to show her the new space poster I got. It glows in the dark!"

I glance at Beth, who's fighting back a grin.

"We're coming in," I say and hang up.

Beth opens her door and steps out, laughing softly. "That was manipulative."

I hand her the to-go bag. "Effective though."

Inside, the house smells like old wood and clean laundry. Gia barrels into the room, barefoot, and snatches the bag from Beth with a shriek of glee. "You're the best. Both of you."

They're already talking as I hang up my keys. By the time I turn around, they're shoulder to shoulder at the kitchen island, fries between them, debating horror movie options.

I hate horror. So of course the two ladies I care the most about would love it.

We settle into the living room. Gia claims the recliner with her chicken burger container. Beth and I take the couch, careful not to crowd each other. Still, our arms touch. Our knees. Every brush feels like a tiny electric shock into my libido.

Gia cues up a space horror flick—Beth claps, delighted.

"My brother hates horror," Gia says with a grin.

"I don't hate it," I protest. "I'm just not a fan of being jump-scared."

"If you get scared," Beth teases, "you can hold my hand."

She does exactly that, wrapping her fingers around mine. Her palm is warm and soft. I don't let go.

We joke. We laugh. Gia throws popcorn at both of us. I feel something inside me unwind.

Halfway through the movie, Gia groans and stretches. "Ugh. I'm wiped."

"You're not gonna finish it?" I ask.

"Seen it like five times." She hugs me, then moves to Beth and hugs her too. "Night. You kids be good."

Beth smiles. "Always."

As soon as Gia's door clicks shut, Beth and I turn to each other.

There's no space left between us—just the warmth of her thigh pressed against mine, the softness of her hair brushing my shoulder when she shifts. Our lips meet, slow and searching. Her fingers rest lightly on my chest, not pulling me closer—just there, warm and real.

We kiss like we're rediscovering something we didn't realize we'd missed. Her hand finds my jaw. Mine slides up her back, slow and deliberate, just under the hem of her sweater. We start to lean in deeper, her body angled toward mine. And then—

-click-

The hallway door swings open and we freeze. Beth straightens just enough to look composed, her hand still resting against my chest. I casually pick up the throw pillow and set it in my lap, to cover anything I don't want seen.

Gia appears in the kitchen in mismatched pajamas, rubbing her eyes. She doesn't look our way. She opens the fridge, grabs a bottle of water, and closes the door with her foot.

Beth leans back, her posture casual but her breath still caught somewhere in her throat.

Gia walks back through the living room, barely noticing us. "This is a good part," she mumbles, glancing at the screen, then disappears down the hall again.

-Click-

Beth lets out a quiet exhale. I glance over and find her watching me, eyes wide with barely-contained laughter.

"We're gonna have to be stealthy," she whispers.

I smile and thread my fingers through hers. "Stealth is one of my many talents."

Beth leans in, brushing her lips against my ear.

"We'll see about that."

When her hand moves over my jeans, I lose the last thread of restraint. I kiss her deeper, feeling her breath catch.

We try to focus on the movie but fail delightfully.

When she swings a leg over me and settles into my lap, my hands grip her hips. Her body against mine is heat and need and heaven.

"How do you feel about your room?" she whispers against my neck.

"What about the movie?" I ask, breathless.

She echoes Gia. "Seen it like five times."

She grinds gently, and I barely hold myself together. "We'd have to be quiet."

"I can be quiet," she murmurs, brushing her lips just below my ear.

I take her hand and lead her down the hall, my whole body on fire. She follows close behind, fingers brushing mine.

Tonight's not about control. It's not about release.

It's about something deeper.

And I don't want to rush a single second.

Forty-One

Stay

―⁂―

Beth

This time, when my head hits the pillow, it's slow and gentle, his hand cradling me as he guides me down. There isn't the intense needy fire there was the last time we found ourselves in bed together. Just softness and anticipation.

Will's other hand is warm against my waist as he leans over me, his lips brushing against mine. The kiss is slow, exploratory but beneath it I feel a growing need. I'm not sure if its his or mine but I hope its both.

When I pull him down with me, he follows, his body heavy and safe over mine. His kisses move to my cheek, my neck, the curve of my collarbone.

"You drive me crazy," he whispers between kisses.

"Good," I breathe.

His fingers find the buttons on my dress and begin to undo them slowly, one at a time. Each pop of thread makes me shiver. When the fabric falls away, his mouth follows, brushing kisses over the exposed skin of my chest, my ribs, the curve beneath my breast.

I run my hands along his shoulders, over the tension in his back. He lets out a soft groan when my fingers find his hair, and I guide his mouth back to mine.

This is different from the first time. It is the furthest from desperate hate sex we could possibly get.

We explore each other like a map we've just been handed—every touch a new discovery. He kisses the inside of my wrist. My jawline. The spot behind my ear that makes me gasp.

His shirt comes off. Mine goes with it. We are slow, but the heat builds with every sigh and touch.

When I shift and pull him beneath me, I watch the way his eyes darken as I straddle him. I lean down, pressing my lips to his ear.

"I want you," I whisper.

He grips my hips, grinding gently. His voice is a low hum. "I want you too."

As we shed the rest of our clothes, our kisses grow deeper, needier—but still quiet. Still careful. Every time a moan threatens, we shush each other with laughter and more kisses.

Will brushes his lips across my breast, murmuring something I can't make out except for the "God, Beth," in the middle.

When I take his cock in my hand, slow and teasing, he shudders. His teeth press to my shoulder like he's about to bite.

He's so warm, so responsive.

We tangle together, sweat-slicked and whispering promises in the dark.

And when it's over—when I finally collapse against his chest, breathless and trembling—he pulls the blanket over us and kisses the top of my head.

"Stay," he whispers. It's a request, not a demand and it sounds so sweet on his lips.

I nestle closer, skin to skin, heart to heart, and close my eyes.

Forty-Two

Taboo, or Not Taboo

Will

Gia's talking a mile a minute as we pull up to Beth's house. She's clutching the party game we picked out earlier like it's a golden ticket. I've got a tray of bakery cookies in one hand, a bottle of wine in the other, and more nerves than I'll admit to anyone.

Beth's been at my place the last few nights. Coming here—this feels like something new. Like showing up *as hers.*

Ben answers the door with a warm smile. I've worked side by side with him the last couple of months. Now I am about to enter this man's abode. It dawns on me how much I respect and admire him as I cross the threshold.

"Hi, Mr. Wilkes!" Gia chirps, all Southern manners and sunshine.

"Gia… you know better than that," he scolds, stepping aside to let us in, "It's Ben."

"Right. Totally." She nods, but after a decade of being raised on 'yes, sir's' and 'no, ma'am's', even calling him Mr. Wilkes is a stretch.

The correction makes me smile.

We follow him into the house, and it's already loud with laughter. The table's surrounded—Missy, Jane, and Chuck, all mid-conversation.

Beth crosses the room, hugs Gia first, then turns to me. Her arms loop around my neck, and I breathe her in—just for a moment longer than necessary. She pulls back, grinning.

"Here, let me take those." She grabs the wine and cookies. "Oooh! Cookies! My favorite."

I glance at Gia, who beams. Her idea. I wink, and she practically vibrates with pride.

Missy comes over and hugs me. It's unexpected but welcome—warm, soft, perfumed with something floral.

"We're glad you two could make it," she says. "Our little game night keeps growing!"

Across the room, Jane coughs behind her hand.

"What?" Beth's mom turns, hands on her hips.

"Nothing," Jane giggles then winks at Beth.

Beth gasps, mock-dramatic. "Oh my god. She is!" Beth's reply to Jane is cryptic, a secret shared between sisters. I'm curious but smart enough to keep my mouth shut. "What kind of subtle sorcery have you been working, Witchy Woman?"

"I have no idea what you're talking about," Missy says, waving them off.

Beth narrows her eyes. "You used to *beg* for boyfriends at the dinner table."

Jane clutches her heart. "Why are you both still single? When will I get grandbabies?" she mimics.

Beth groans. "Nope, we're done here."

I stand there, grinning like a fool, watching it all unfold. The teasing. The timing. The affection underneath all of it. I thought my family could stir it up—but this is something entirely different, laced with affection, not expectations. This is *home*.

Chuck raises an eyebrow and nods my way. "You doing alright?"

"Just observing," I say. "You all could sell tickets."

Beth brings me a glass of wine while Missy leads Gia to the fridge for a soda. We pick out the kind of party game that breaks into chaos fast. Taboo.

Teams are uneven, so Missy insists on watching from the sidelines, making the split Me, Gia, and Beth and Jane, Chuck, and Ben.

I quickly learn just how competitive the Wilkes Family is as my mind seems to lag just a second behind each of them. Beth and Gia are a deadly combo though, reading ach other like a book, so they keep the points rolling in.

We're two points behind when it's my turn to close the gap. *Mine. Mr. Tongue-Tied All Night.*

First card's easy. "And you get a car!"

"Oprah!" Beth's mom shouts from the sidelines.

Jane groans. "Mom, *you're not playing!*"

I shrug. "I'll take it."

Second card, tougher. I manage to get Gia to guess *Rollerblade*. Her face lights up when she gets it, like I just handed her a trophy.

I draw a third card and laugh. This one's a gift.

I look at Beth. "Meet cute."

She hesitates for half a second, then her face splits into a grin.

"Coffee!" she shouts.

I toss the card face-up. No more needed. The round ends, we win. But all I care about was that look from Beth.

The laughter winds down as we drift toward the kitchen for snacks. I check my phone while refilling my drink.

A new email sits at the top of my inbox:

SUBJECT: Estate Determination – Private Holdings Clarified

It's from Gregory.

I read it quickly—then again, slower.

Will,

Catherine Fitzgerald cannot withhold your inheritance. Your portion of your father's estate was separated from the broader family trust and is legally yours, uncontested. If you choose to walk away from the Fitzgerald trust, you retain full rights to your share. I've included documents for disbursement.

Best,

Gregory

The glass is cool in my hand, but heat rises to my chest. I walk back into the living room and raise my voice enough to quiet the room.

"Hey. Uh, can I get your attention for a sec?"

Their heads turn and I find myself in the limelight. Beth's brow lifts, Gia pauses mid-sip of soda.

"I just heard from Gregory," I say. "The estate lawyer."

Jane winces like she's bracing for a bomb.

But I smile. "It's good news. Cathy can't block our inheritance. Gia and I are in the clear."

There's a beat of silence before Gia gasps, wide-eyed. "You're serious?"

"Bout damn time!" Beth exhales as though she knew it was coming any day.

Then Missy claps. Chuck lets out a low whistle.

I nod still drunk with relief. "Totally. It's ours. No strings, no leverage, no Cathy."

Gia whoops and jumps up from the couch, doing a ridiculous little dance across the living room floor.

"Freedom dance!" She sings. "This is my rich girl happy jig!"

Everyone laughs. Beth doubles over, wiping tears from her eyes. Even Ben grins as he lifts his drink.

"To building your own legacy," he says.

We all raise our glasses, soda cans, or cookies. It's silly, chaotic, and perfect.

Beth leans into my side, voice low. "You good?"

I nod. "I'm great."

She kisses me softly, just a little peck, but it's warm and loving.

Ben laughs, breaking the spell between us. "You're doing alright by Beth and that's more important to me than any inheritance in the world."

"Still," Gia puts in, "I'm not gonna complain about the money!"

Beth looks up at me and smiles.

"You ready for another round?" she asks.

"With this family?" I grin. "Absolutely."

Forty-Three

A Girl and Her Horse

Beth

Dancer picks up speed beneath me, stretching into an easy lope beside Gia and Gypsy. Our horses move in rhythm over the packed earth, the late afternoon sun painting everything in gold. The air smells like warm sage and distant cedar, the kind of scent that soaks into your skin and makes you feel like you belong to the land.

Gia rides like she was born in that saddle—posture tall, reins loose, her movements fluid and instinctive. There's no hesitation in her. She's all confidence and grace, and Gypsy mirrors her energy like they're sharing a single heartbeat.

Bowie darts ahead of us through the brush, tail high, a flash of white against the fall-colored scrub. He stops to sniff something, then zips back toward us, ears perked like he's making sure we're still behind him.

We've been out here for a while now—winding beyond the property, into the trails crisscrossing at the mountain's commanding base. I hadn't planned this ride to be anything special, but something about it feels like it is.

"You ever just… wish you could stay out here forever?" Gia's voice is soft, her eyes forward.

"Most days," I say.

She smiles, but it fades quickly. "I keep thinking about what Cathy said."

As the trail widens, I slow Dancer to align next to Gia and Gyps. The horse flicks an ear back at me but stays relaxed. "She get to you?"

Gia shrugs. "Yeah, I know she's full of it. Doesn't mean it doesn't mess with my head. Like… one screw-up and poof—everything's gone. She treats us like we're her clones.. Or clowns! Puppets on a string!."

"She's wrong," I say, quiet but firm. "But I know that kind of fear. It stops people twice your age or more, right in their tracks. You're a brave girl!."

Gia watches the trail ahead. "What if I mess this up? What if we lose it anyway?"

I let the silence stretch for a few beats, letting the wind speak while I find the right words.

"I've lost everything before," I say.

She turns to look at me, startled. "You have?"

I nod. "Back in San Francisco, I had the whole picture. Big job, apartment, relationship. On paper, it looked perfect. But inside? I was shrinking every day. My ex… he was the kind of person who made you feel lucky just to be tolerated."

Gia's eyes widen. She opens her mouth, then closes it again.

"I finally walked out with an apartment worth of crap and a sliver of savings. No plan, no backup. Just came back to stay with my parents and put myself back together."

"And now you run a whole therapy business."

I smile. "Turns out, burning down the wrong life makes space for the right one."

We ride quietly for a moment, the horses navigating the trail with the kind of ease that only comes from trust.

"You think Will and I are doing the right thing?" she asks.

"I do," I say. "You're building something that matters. Cathy might have money, but she doesn't have what you two have. And she knows it."

Gia smiles and looks away.

Gypsy flicks her tail and stretches her neck as Gia strokes her gently.

"Gypsy and I are buds. She's like my spirit animal."

"Yeah she is," I agree.

Gia tilts her head, watching Gypsy's ears flick at the wind. "She's, like... kind of amazing."

I smile. "She's got something, that's for sure. Just like you."

"She's gonna make a good therapy horse," Gia adds, giving Gypsy a light scratch on the neck.

I nod, but I'm already thinking it. *Maybe not in the way I imagined.* Not a horse shuffled between clients every hour. She's not built to tolerate, but to connect. She's loyal and sensitive.

"She's got a big heart," I say instead. "So, what about you? Found yourself a horse of your own yet?"

"Nah. Not the right one." She pats Gypsy's shoulder. "But when I do... I hope she's like Gyps."

She showed me her chicks yesterday and they'd picked up the cutest goats last week that she still gushes over. I think I know why she hasn't picked out a horse.

My chest pulls tight. The wind catches Gypsy's mane and flicks it across Gia's arm like a ribbon. They're in sync. Of course they are.

"I'm sure she will be." I know what I'm going to do. The seed had been planted months ago but our occasional afternoon rides have really shown how bonded the two are. I'm going to call Will and see about giving one stubborn beautiful heart to another.

* * *

That evening, I find Will on the porch, beer in hand, staring out across the land like he's trying to memorize every inch.

I sit beside him without asking.

"I've been thinking," I say, "about Gypsy. And Gia."

He glances at me, curious.

"I want to give her the horse. Officially."

His expression softens, a slow curve of pride behind his eyes. "She'd love that."

"I just… wanted your blessing."

He turns to face me fully. "Beth, anything that makes Gia feel chosen, seen, loved—do it. No hesitation."

I smile, unexpected tears pricking my eyes. "You're a good brother."

He shrugs, but I see the emotion flicker there.

"I feel like it used to be easy," he says.

"Nothing worth doing is easy."

I lean into him and rest my head against his shoulder. The stars come out one by one above us, and Bowie flops down at our feet with a huff. The ranch sprawls under the open sky, peaceful and nearly whole. Now to make plans to move a horse in.

Forty-Four

This One's Got Heart

Beth

The autumn air smells like damp hay and the faint sweetness of horse feed. I stand just outside the barn office, a manila folder tucked beneath my arm, Bowie trotting faithfully at my side. From the far end of the property, I hear the rhythmic thud of a hammer as someone finishes mounting the new sign—soft greens and purples brushed into flowing script across fresh cedar. *Healing Spirit: Equine Therapy & Wellness.*

Six months ago, I was running home to lick my wounds in this valley. Now, I'm standing tall and planting roots.

I push the office door open.

Carol is waiting inside, leaning against the desk like she's been here all along. Her reading glasses are perched on her nose and a grin is already tugging at her cheeks.

"Well," she says, taking the glasses off, "you ready to make it yours?"

I exhale, slow and steady. "Yeah. I really am."

I lay the folder on the desk and flip it open. One signature after another. Transfer of ownership. Client list. Stable. Horses still in rotation. Every scribble of ink feels surreal.

When I finish, Carol slides a glass of something amber and bubbly toward me. "The old girl's all yours, sweetheart. Make sure to always remind her who's boss."

I laugh—light, a little disbelieving. "God, it's real. It's mine."

Carol raises her glass. "To stubborn women, good horses, and taking the reins."

We clink, drink, and sit in the quiet together for one more moment, letting it settle. Letting *me* settle.

Eventually, she pushes away from the desk. "I do not envy you."

"I'm sure you don't. Retirement already looks good on you. Not that you're going to slow down an inch." I raise my cup to the air again and take another sip.

She winks. "Now when I come to bail your ass out on paperwork or horse shoeing, I'll be the employee. Damn. Never thought I'd see the day."

"Oh, I plan to make your life *very* difficult."

"Thatta girl."

She slips out the door, leaving me alone in the office I now own. I glance at the certification on the wall. A doctorate, and now an equine assisted therapist certification. I take a long, slow walk down the length of the therapy barn, Bowie close to my heels. Dust floats in the late afternoon light like golden motes of memory. I pass by Cocoa's stall, then Hanzels, to the empty stalls where Pepper and Biscuit once rested their noses, begging for carrots. The stable is quieter without them, but I know one day I'll have it full again. Gyspy was going to occupy one of those stalls, but I've had a change of heart and I know where she is going will be so much better for her.

I stop in the center of the barn and take a deep breath.

"It's mine," I whisper.

Bowie wags his tail. I swear, he understands.

* * *

By sundown, the barn has transformed. String lights sway gently above the paddock, casting a warm glow across hay bales and folding tables. Carol dubbed it a *Changing of the Guard* BBQ, and somehow the name stuck.

Ben and Will are at the grill—Ben barking directions, Will pretending not to listen. Chuck lounges near the food table, beer in hand, while Jane corrals napkins before they blow away. Carol's in full host mode, bouncing between guests and handing out cider like it's currency. The whole community seems to be here—clients, neighbors, friends. It's the kind of evening that hits me right in my soul.

Although I could do without public speeches. When Carol ushers me over, my stomach twists.

"Remind me why I agreed to this again?" I murmur to Carol as we stand near the fire pit.

"Because you like free burgers and public praise," she says, bumping my shoulder. "Also, you earned this."

"I could've gone without the whole toast thing."

"Nonsense. You're the woman of the hour. Bask in it."

And thus, the toasting hour has arrived. Carol clinks a spoon to her glass and raises it high.

"Everyone!" she calls. "Thank you for coming out to celebrate this major milestone. I've had the honor of running Healing Spirit for a good stretch of time, and today, I pass the reins to someone who's earned them the hard way. With grit, grace, and an ungodly amount of early mornings. I'm telling ya this woman even got up before the sun to help me chase down my retirement fund."

Laughter ripples through the crowd.

"I could not be prouder to see Beth take over this place—and lucky for me, I get to stick around and work *for* her now."

I raise an eyebrow. "Edict one: a strict dress code."

"Oh, I'll wear your logo proudly."

Ben steps forward next, holding a cider bottle like a microphone. "I've watched this young woman work her tail off since she was little. She came back, stood tall, and built something meaningful. And I'll tell you right now—Healing Spirit couldn't be in better hands."

I swallow against the lump in my throat. Everyone turns to me.

No pressure.

I step up, heart thudding. "Thank you all—for believing in this place, and in me. I came back here thinking I'd start over quietly. Maybe rebuild my practice. I didn't expect community. I didn't expect so much love. But I'm grateful beyond words."

I hold up my glass. "To second chances, wild horses, and finding home when you least expect it."

The crowd claps, cheers. Carol squeezes my shoulder before melting back into the party.

A moment later, Will pulls me aside near the fence line.

"That was a hell of a speech," he says.

"You helped build it, you know. Or, well, rebuild it."

He shrugs. "I just held the drill."

He steps a little closer. "I meant it before. I'm proud of you."

I look at him, really look, and it hits me again. The man I judged when he first rolled into town is standing beside me now like an anchor I didn't know I needed.

"I know," I whisper. "I'm proud of you too."

From behind us, Gia appears with a plate of apple pie and a huge grin.

"I've finally decided on the name," she says, bouncing on her heels.

"What name?" I ask.

"For the ranch. The new one. When it's ready."

Will raises an eyebrow. "I thought we were keeping it a secret."

Gia leans in and whispers it in my ear.

It's perfect. Warmth floods my chest.

"We are." She says and puts her arm over my shoulder.

"I love it," I say, hugging her.

"We're saving the big reveal for the grand opening," she adds with a conspiratorial wink.

Will holds his hands up. "Gia decided it couldn't be anything with 'Fitzgerald' in it. I agreed."

"All due respect to your ancestors," I chime in, "but the name now is a bit… formal."

Gia laughs. "Exactly. This one's got *heart*."

And as I look at them—Will, Gia, Bowie rolling in the grass nearby—I realize she's right. Two little words with so much meaning and promise. I can't wait to see it revealed.

Forty-Five

A Moment In the Sun

Beth

It's August now. Summer's still stretching its legs, but with school back in session, the beaches are starting to clear. Tourists have returned to their regular lives, leaving Lake Tahoe's quieter shores for the locals.

Gia just started her freshman year at Douglas High and—no surprise—she's already made a few friends. The girl could talk her way into NASA if she wanted to. Hell, she probably will. But for now, she's juggling school, slowly building a new social circle that exists beyond Discord and memories of Newport Beach, and helping Will bring the ranch vision to life.

Will's been on site nearly every day, pushing the cabins through final inspection and overseeing the last-minute details. The vegetable garden's planted and thriving. A local landscape team has transformed the dusty stretch beyond the barn into something beautiful but still raw—a sagebrush maze with a desert Zen garden at its center. I can't walk through it without hearing Carol's voice say, "You're really leaning into wellness, huh?"

And as for me? Healing Spirit is mine, fully and officially. Carol's off exploring retirement with a renewed passport, and I've taken over both the business and the house. It's a big shift—living alone again—but I like it.

Will and Gia's place is only a few minutes away, and we spend most of our evenings together anyway. Gia's grown on me more than I expected. She's part friend, part little sister, part chaos goblin.

Bowie's doubled in size since I adopted him. He may technically be mine, but he's become a family dog—equal parts therapy animal, adventure buddy, and emotional sponge.

He barrels across the sand now, chasing Gia toward the waterline. She shrieks, laughing, then spins and splashes into the lake, egging him on. It's one of those perfectly ordinary moments that somehow lodges deep in your chest.

I glance at Will beside me, lounging back on the blanket, eyes squinting at the horizon. I wonder what he's thinking. Before I can ask, he looks over and catches me staring. His smile is lazy, content, and when he leans in, I meet him halfway.

I pull back just enough to press my hand to his chest.

"Tag," I say, voice low. "You're it."

I burst up and bolt for the safety of Tahoe's icy waters. The sun catching the water ahead of me, cold spray waiting, the sound of his laughter close behind.

Forty-Six

Party Planner Extraordinaire

Beth

I'm elbow-deep in folding chair math, clipboard tucked under one arm, trying to solve a last-minute layout problem. The seating diagram went missing twenty minutes ago—possibly to the wind, possibly sabotage—and now I'm winging it. Controlled chaos. But chaos nonetheless.

"Three inches apart," I mutter. "Just enough for booties and elbows."

Out of the corner of my eye, Will leans against the stall post, watching me with a stupid soft smile that makes my pulse hiccup. He's covered in sweat and dirt and confidence. Its nice to see him believing that this is all going to work.

The barn looks incredible. Gia's banners are up, Jane and Chuck are setting out tables, Missy's commanding teenagers with more flair than a Vegas stage mom, and somewhere in all this, I forgot to eat lunch, drink water, or notice the sky. Doesn't matter.

I'm not an owner here. This isn't my ranch. But I want it to succeed like it is. So charts and checklists be damned, I keep at it until everything looks just right.

Will and I trade a glance across the barn. It's brief, but heavy with something I've come to recognize—an electric heat, mutual respect, maybe something even scarier than that.

Gia jogs up from the paddock, cheeks pink and ponytail bouncing. "Banners are up. Water barrels filled. Chuck confirmed hay bale delivery. We're locked and loaded."

"Rockstar," I tell her.

"Wait until Will sees the flyer I printed," she says, waggling her brows.

"You didn't."

"Oh, I did. Full moody cowboy glory."

Will groans. "Why are there even photos of that?"

"Because Jane has no chill," Gia fires back.

We all laugh, and it fills me up—this strange, perfect group of people who've become something like a family. Maybe exactly that.

Will steps beside me, gaze sweeping over everything. "This looks incredible."

"Because of you," I say automatically.

He shakes his head. "Because of you. You have an eye for this kind of thing, Beth Wilkes."

I want to deny it, but the words lodge somewhere in my throat. All I can do is smile and maybe blush just a little.

Then Gia is back with her phone. "Look! Front page spread tomorrow!"

The photo makes me freeze. It's the one I took—just for fun, I said. The ranch at sunrise. Painted fencing, gravel drive, golden light on the house, guest cabins glowing in the distance.

Will lets out a long 'ooooh.'

Gia looks up, softer now. "This is really happening."

He nods. "Then we better make sure it's unforgettable."

I tick a box on my clipboard. "Hey Gia, can you grab me more masking tape?"

I wait until she's run off then turn to Will, "Speaking of unforgettable… I've been thinking about Gypsy."

His brow lifts. "Oh?"

"She and Gia… they've really bonded."

"She talks about Gypsy non-stop." he says.

"I was thinking maybe… what if you give her to Gia? As a gift. For tomorrow."

He grins. "Funny. I was thinking of asking if I could buy her off you."

I smirk. "You think your money's any good here?"

"Nope. And I'm gonna let you take credit."

"How about making her from *us*?"

He leans in and kisses my forehead. "Thank you. I just know how much it'll mean to her. Let's move her over together."

We trade grins, plotting like kids about to surprise Santa. It's gonna take a good plan and a fair amount of luck to keep it a secret until the Grand Opening.

Ben passes behind us, slaps Will on the back. "You've done well here." He nods to me, then disappears like a ghost in the night.

Gia returns with her notepad and field-commander energy, handing me the tape without even looking up. "Okay. Fire pit rules, raffle schedule, cider flow…"

She pauses. Her eyes narrow.

"What?" I ask.

"You two are smiling way too much."

"We're up to something," I say sweetly.

"Ew. Don't tell me." She fake-gags, which only makes us laugh harder.

We knock out the last checklist items just as the sun drops behind the ridge. The volunteers filter out. Chuck and Jane head home. Ben and Missy leave with waves and parting jokes. The cabins catch that last kiss of gold like something out of a magazine.

It's just the three of us now. Me, Will, and Gia. Our little found family.

Funny, a few months ago, I was gutting out the first chapter of a lonely restart. I didn't expect to fall in love with a ranch. Or a teenage girl. Or a man who makes my heart quiet and loud at the same time.

But here we are.

Inside, we make cocoa. Extra marshmallows for Gia. We sit on the porch steps in quiet communion while the world winds down.

Forty-Seven

It's Happening For Real

Will

The smell of barbecue drifts through the air, thick with sage and mesquite, wrapping around the sound of music and the buzz of conversation. String lights dangle from fence posts. Kids dart between hay bales. People I barely know call me by name.

It's happening. For real.

I grip the paper cup of cider in my hand and scan the ranch—*our* ranch—now buzzing with life. Cabins polished to a shine. Art installations tucked along the trails. Handmade signage Gia insisted on hand painting. It's a damn miracle.

Beth stands to my left, clipboard tucked under one arm, wind lifting her hair slightly as she smiles at the crowd. She's glowing, not just from the sunset, but from the kind of pride that doesn't need to be spoken out loud.

"I still can't believe we pulled this off," I say.

Beth bumps my shoulder. "Believe it. It's beautiful."

I take a breath. "So are you."

She raises a brow. "Smooth."

I meet her eyes with my own and wink. She giggles and turns away.

Gia bursts through the crowd before Beth can tease me more. She's flushed from the heat, hair windblown, and eyes bright with excitement.

"They're ready," she says. "I'm going up."

I nod, and the three of us make our way toward the stage. Beth squeezes my hand once before letting go.

Gia hops onto the hay bale we've designated as the "podium," clears her throat, and grabs the mic. The noise quiets fast. People listen when Gia talks.

"Hi, I'm Gia," she starts. "If you don't know me, I'm the boss of this place. Just kidding. Sort of."

Laughter breaks the tension, and she grins.

"Okay, so... a year ago I was a total mess. I'd lost everything I knew, and I came here thinking I'd just hide out while my brother figured out our lives. But something weird happened. People here didn't treat me like a guest or a charity case. They treated me like I mattered. Even when I was snappy or awkward or bossy—which, let's be honest, I still kinda am."

More laughter. She shifts her weight, then continues.

"I didn't know what this ranch could be when we bought it. Honestly? I think I just wanted something to hold on to. Something that was mine. But it turns out, this place isn't about *me*. It's about all of us. Everyone who showed up to build fence or bake cookies or tell me I was being ridiculous and then hug me anyway."

She glances at Beth. Then me. Her voice wavers, just slightly.

"I miss my parents every day. But I think... if they could see me now, they'd be proud." She choked on the words, then stopped to take a deep breath. When she continued, her voice quivered. "Not because this is big, or pretty, or successful—but because I *chose* it. Because I didn't give up."

She flips a sheet of paper off the covered sign, revealing the new name: **Sunrise and Sagebrush.**

Applause erupts. Cameras flash. Gia beams, but she looks at us like we're her whole world. And honestly? Right now, we kind of are.

Beth leans in beside me, voice soft. "So, City Slicker... what are *you* going to do when she takes it over?"

I watch Gia hug Carol, then Jane, then a bewildered toddler with a juice box.

"I don't know," I say. "Figure it out as I go."

Beth arches a brow.

"But whatever I build next…" I reach for her hand. "It's gonna be alongside the people who matter. That's the part I know for sure."

Her fingers intertwine with mine.

I look at the crowd, the ranch, the way the sign glows in the dying light.

Sunrise and Sagebrush. Funny how a place I once saw as a burden now feels like the one place I don't want to leave.

* * *

Beth

An hour later the food's mostly gone. The band plays their last song. People are scattering into small groups or headed back to their cars. That's when I tug Gia's hand.

"Hey," I whisper. "Come with me."

She narrows her eyes. "Am I in trouble?"

"Not even close."

I lead her toward the barn, away from the crowd, the air quieter and cooler here. I pause outside one of the stables.

"Remember how you said you hadn't found your horse yet?"

She nods slowly.

I reach for the latch. "Actually, that's not true. You found her months ago."

For a moment Gia looks confused, but then her eyes go wide as she peeks through the stable doors.

Inside, Gypsy lifts her head, ears twitching. The stall is fresh—new water, her familiar hay, and a nameplate tucked in the hay with Gia's name scrawled across the bottom.

Gia's mouth drops open. "What? No. No way."

I smile. "Will and I agreed. She belongs with you."

She takes one bouncing step forward. "Oh my God... are you serious?" Her body is quivering in anticipation.

"Dead serious."

"Holy crap." She turns to me, voice cracking. "This is, like... I don't even have words. She's *perfect.*"

"She chose you, Gia. It was always her call."

She jumps into my arms and I wrap her up in a bear hug. She pulls Will in as well and the three of us embrace as Gypsy snorts, reminding us she's still there, too. Gia let's go and approaches the mare, gently stroking her nose.

"I'm gonna cry," she says, even as she tries to laugh it off.

"I won't tell anyone."

Later, I find Will at the edge of the bonfire circle, watching Gia lead Gypsy across the darkening paddock. The flames cast a soft glow against the sky. Laughter floats across the clearing. The cabins stand tall behind us, solid and warm.

Will glances at me. "She looks happy."

"She is."

He slips an arm around my shoulders, and I lean into him. My chest is full—of pride, of gratitude, of something I'm not quite ready to name.

This place isn't mine. But it feels like home.

Forty-Eight

Something Real

Will

The house is quiet except for the tick of the kitchen clock and the occasional creak of old wood settling into the night. Beth leans against the doorway, her arms folded, the softest smile on her lips. Her boots are off. Her hair's a little messy. She looks like everything I've ever needed and never knew to ask for.

Bowie's passed out in his bed, dead to the world after a day full of chasing kids and dropped hot dogs. Gia conked out an hour ago. The ranch is silent after a long, incredible day of celebration. As happy as I was to see so many come out to support our grand opening, I am even more happy they're all gone.

Beth raises an eyebrow. "We did it."

I nod, stepping closer. "You did it."

She snorts. "I'm pretty sure your blisters have blisters."

"Yeah," I say. "And I'd do it all again."

We meet in the middle of the room. She rests her forehead against my chest and I wrap my arms around her like it's instinct. Like I've been doing this forever. Her body molds into mine, soft curves against hard lines, and for a moment we just stand there, swaying slightly, exhausted but content.

"We should go to bed," she murmurs.

"Bed sounds good."

"Sleep sounds better."

I chuckle, low and rough. "Yeah, well. I'm so tired my bones hurt."

She leans back to look up at me. "Then what are you still doing standing here?"

I let my eyes drift down her body, slow and deliberate. "Because no amount of exhaustion is going to keep me from getting my hands on you."

The flush that rises in her cheeks is everything. I press a kiss to her temple, then her jaw, then lower. I draw her mouth to mine, teasing her with my tongue before pulling away and tugging her hand in the direction of my bedroom.

We make our way down the hallway, brushing shoulders, fingers tangling as we go. The weight of the day hangs over us, but it's fading with every touch. By the time we reach the bedroom, there's nothing left but the heat building between us.

She kisses me first, slow and soft. I deepen it, pressing my body against hers. Her fingers slide beneath my shirt, skimming skin, and I groan into her mouth. That lazy tension between us ignites in an instant.

Her hands tangle in my hair as I lift her gently onto the bed, our mouths parting just long enough to breathe. We're tired. We should be asleep. But with her beneath me, skin warm and golden in the lamplight, sleep is the last thing on my mind.

"Just a quick one," she teases, voice husky.

I smirk, lips brushing her collarbone. "No such thing with you."

She arches into me, and I feel the ripple of her breath, the anticipation humming beneath her skin. We move slower this time, deliberately—kisses stretching long and lingering.

Her laugh melts into a moan as my hand trails up her thigh, her body already soft and open for me. She's fire under my palms, a promise I want to keep all night. I press two fingers into her, relishing her moan.

"Beth," I whisper.

She meets my gaze, her voice steady. "I want you."

I close my eyes for a beat, grounding myself. This isn't just arousal—it's need, fierce and anchoring.

The rest of our clothes come off in a slow tangle of limbs and low murmurs. She pulls me back down to her, lips finding mine, and we fall into rhythm like the world outside doesn't exist.

I grab the length of my cock, stroking it as I rub it along her. I feel how wet she is and it takes all my self control not to thrust into her. I tease her- and myself- until she grabs my hips and thrusts her pelvis toward mine. With a moan that is part growl, I sink into her, slow and deep.

She wraps her legs around me like I belong to her. And I do, entirely. We move together, bodies finding their own language, laughter giving way to breathless moans and whispered names. I pump in and out of her as I kiss her neck and nibble the tips of her perfect breasts, making her back arch in a way I never get sick of.

She's soft and strong and completely, impossibly mine. Her breath catches, her body tightens around me, and I follow her into that perfect place where nothing else matters. As she reaches orgasm, tightening impossibly around my cock, I press my face into the pillow next to hers and pump harder and faster until I am releasing into her.

Afterward, we lie tangled in each other, sweat cooling on our skin, the sheets kicked halfway to the floor. Her head rests on my chest, her fingers tracing slow circles across my ribs.

I stare at the ceiling, one arm slung around her shoulders, and feel something in me settle. Like I've finally stopped running.

"This," I murmur, "is the part they don't tell you about."

She hums. "The part where everything's messy and sticky and smells like sex?"

"Exactly."

"We should be asleep."

"We will be. Eventually."

She tilts her head up, eyes gleaming. "Worth staying up for."

I grin, pull her closer. "Every damn time."

Forty-Nine

Another Sunrise

Beth

The goats get to arguing before the rooster even thinks about crowing. That's the kind of place this is now. Birds began their singing well before Bowie had nuzzled his way into my armpit to coax me up for walkies. And all of this was before the sun, who is now showing his radiant crown over the eastern ridge of the valley.

I sit on the porch swing in my favorite knit sweater and a pair of Will's thick socks, hands wrapped around my coffee mug like it's sacred. I take in a long, deep breath as a slow pink stretches across the horizon, promising a bright, if crisp, day to come.

Bowie flops at my feet with a long, satisfied dog sigh. We've already walked the property once this morning. He chased a rabbit he had no chance of catching, I threatened a goat who thought my boot laces were edible, and I slipped in mud that was *definitely* not just mud. It was, in short, a perfect morning.

From here I can see the outline of the guest cabins just beginning to catch light. There's frost on the roof shingles and a few puffs of chimney smoke curling into the air—some of Gia's guests are early risers so Bowie and I have already shared several 'good mornings' before I directed them to the main house for coffee and a continental breakfast.

Guests. It still blows me away. I'd checked the booking app and turns out the ranch is booked through spring. Who knew "desert snow getaways" would be such a successful marketing angle? Apparently Gia is well on the way to making *Sunrise and Sagebrush* the hot new escape.

The kitchen light flicks on behind me. I don't turn around, but I smile.

Will appears a few minutes later, rubbing a hand through his hair. He's got that heavy-sleep dazed look, like his brain hasn't caught up to his body yet. He holds out his mug without a word. I toast him with my own.

"Morning," he mumbles, sitting beside me.

"So I see," I smirk.

We sit in silence, sipping coffee, watching the sun finally tip over the ridge. He nestles his head onto my shoulder.

"You know," I say, "we probably should've called it *Blisters and Band-Aids*."

He chuckles, low and warm. "Not as marketable."

"Fair."

We don't need words, not really. After the last few weeks—the boom of bookings post-press, the hiccups with plumbing in cabin three, the couple who brought an untrained great pyrenees as an emotional support animal—it's enough just to breathe together.

Later, we'll have a full day: a therapy session in the arena, a local news team coming to do a follow-up piece, dinner with Chuck and Jane. But right now, it's just us, caffeine, and the goats still arguing with the chickens like they own the place.

Sometimes, after dinner, we fold laundry together. He holds up the underwear like it's top-secret intel and I threaten to replace all his socks with neon ones. Sometimes we don't even make it to bed before we're tangled up in each other, laughing into the creaking floorboards. Other nights, we fall asleep shoulder to shoulder on the couch, the dog curled between us like he's supervising.

There's no ring. No official talk of the future. Just this steady, quiet rhythm we've found—two people who built something real and decided to stay in it, day by day.

Will finishes his coffee and sets the mug down.

"I've got something for you," he says.

I raise a brow. "Better not be another goat."

"Tempting. But no."

He reaches into the pocket of his flannel and pulls out a keyring. There are two old brass keys and a tiny wooden tag shaped like a cabin. It says *#1: Sagebrush Suite*. That's our secret code for his bedroom and the keys look an awful lot like the main house keys.

I take it, fingers brushing his.

"It's yours," he says. "Whenever you want it. No pressure. No expectations."

I turn it over in my hand.

"I can still keep my place?"

"Absolutely. You want your space, you keep it. But if you want mine too… it's yours."

The porch swing creaks as I lean over and kiss him—soft, sure, full of everything we haven't needed to say out loud.

"Thanks," I whisper. "Not just for these," I hold up the keyring, "but for everything. For being that cute, charming cowboy at the coffee shop. And for being so much more than that."

He grins. "I guess it was a good idea I skipped Starbucks."

"Yeah," I answer simply, leaning into him.

The sun's fully up now, casting golden light over the dirt, the cabins, the fencing Will built alongside my dad, and the sagebrush maze that has gone grey as the bushes prepare for the bitter cold of winter. Sunrises and Sagebrush, the two things that brought Gia to this ranch in the first place, and the perfect name for a legacy.

This life isn't perfect. And I would never call it easy. But it's beautiful, complete, and ours.

Fifty

Epilogue

~~~~~~~~~~~~~~~~~~~~~~

Gia

Dear Mom and Dad,

It's been two years since the accident. That number feels weird to write down. Some days it feels like it just happened. Some days it feels like you've been gone forever. Today, it feels like both.

It's also been a year and a half since we opened the ranch. <u>My ranch.</u> Still sounds crazy, right? I mean, a fourteen-year-old pitching business plans to my brother like it was Shark Tank! Now the guest cabins are booked through next month. The petting zoo is oth! Even the garden actually grows stuff! And people come here—like on purpose—to unplug and connect and ride horses and paint rocks and do all the things I used to dream about when everything felt too hard.

I still miss you every single day. I miss Mom's perfume and how she'd sing badly on purpose just to make me laugh. I miss Dad's stupid dad-jokes and his way of pretending he didn't cry at movies when we definitely saw him do it. I miss the way we fit—our three-person team, messy and perfect.

...Sorry for the wet spots. I got all teary, but I'm okay now. More than okay.

Will's doing great. He's not just "holding it together" anymore—he's my fun big brother again. His shoulders don't slouch the way you used to tell me not to

Sunrises and Sagebrush

and he laughs way more. He and Beth are like... a whole thing now. Like two trees growing next to each other, roots all tangled up. It's kinda gross and kinda beautiful. I love them both so much it hurts.

Beth gets me, though. More than almost anyone. We ride together. Bake together. She taught me to make homemade pasta and how to set boundaries. (Not sure which skill is more useful, tbh.)

She gave me this journal, by the way. Last year when I came back from visiting you guys. She said it was to talk to you whenever I want to. I used to write in it all the time. Sorry I don't as much anymore. I still think about you guys like crazy!!

Also—friends. I have them. Lilah from the community garden has basically adopted me into her weird little friend group. We meet at the coffee shop for trivia nights and volunteer events. And guess what? Bella and Tamsin visited from back home. They were obsessed. Lilah and the others loved them. It was this crazy, perfect mix of my old life and my new one, and I didn't even realize how badly I needed that until it happened.

So yeah. I still cry sometimes. I still get scared. I still wish things were different. But I also laugh so hard I snort, and ride Gypsy like we were born in sync, and fall asleep knowing I'm safe, and loved, and home.

And today? Big day. I finally turned sixteen a couple days ago. I am about to take my driver's license test. I know! Terrifying, right? Pray to the DMV gods for me.

Anyway—I gotta go. Will's yelling something about parallel parking and Beth's saying we're late.

Love you both. Always.

—Gia

I twirl a heart up around my name, then wiggle the pen back into the little elastic loop. I take a deep breath before closing the journal and setting it gently on the bedside table next to a photo of Mom and Dad—Mom's arms are wrapped around Dad's and they're both laughing into the camera. It's my favorite picture of them.

I hear Beth call from outside, "Giaaa! Grab your paperwork!"

"I'm coming!" I shout back, grabbing my denim jacket and bolting for the

Epilogue

door.

And just like that—I run toward adulthood with reckless abandon. I'm Gia. Sunrises and Sagebrush is mine and so is the rest of my entire future. Starting with my driver's license.

Made in the USA
Las Vegas, NV
08 June 2025